THE GREAT
SILENT ROAR

THE GREAT
SILENT ROAR

Jordan Castro

Cover artist: Ricardo Roig
Editor: Mari Ciampini.

Print information available on the last page.

Rev. date: 06/14/2021

To order additional copies of this book, contact:
Xlibris
844-714-8691
www.Xlibris.com
Orders@Xlibris.com
825841

DEDICATION

Thank you, God, for enabling me to do this again. So many have lost so much during the time it took me to write this novel and I have counted my abundant blessings by hand.

To my son Caiden, meaning 'battler, fighter.' Son, we came so close to losing you and I cherish every breath you take. The fight in you inspires me to fight too. You put the 'Jax' in 'Jaxton,' my beautiful boy. This book is my gift to you.

To my daughter, Evangeline. Your wit, charm and charisma give me life. You are the manifestation of God's grace in my life, and you are the 'Grace' in this novel.

To my incredible wife, Angelique. The year we met is the year the ascent began. Eight straight years of 'live, love, laugh.' All my happiest moments are with you closely by my side.

Always, to my parents, Rose and Reinaldo. There is no greater comfort in life than the safety net of 'Mom and Dad.' Thank you for always having your door open and the coffee on the stove. I love you both dearly.

To my siblings, Shanna and David, who have always driven me. Being the middle child is easy when you are flanked by two great minds. I love you both; together, we rise.

Thank you, Ricardo Roig, for channeling Gatsby and Van Gogh in this gorgeous cover. And thank you to his sister—and my editor—Mari Ciampini, for all the red pen marks on the page. You pushed me to be so much better.

To my platoon at the 32nd Precinct in Harlem. If they saw everything you did, they would never use the word 'defund' again. You are the heroes that little kids are searching for. See you at roll call.

To Sergeant Galileo Garcia, may God rest your soul. To Detective Cedrick Dixon, may God rest your soul. The NYPD is hurting without you. We miss you.

To my friend, Harold, in Heaven. Nearly twice my age and more than twice my exuberance. I regret not stopping you in the streets when I saw you during the height of the pandemic. I wrote you into this book so you can live forever in literature.

To anyone experiencing darkness and depression, whose daily cries go unanswered because they are released in a frequency the rest of us can't hear—this novel is for you. We know you are roaring. We know the roar is silent. Make us hear you. We care deeply about you. Your lives matter.

In 'The Great Silent Roar,' I (once again) 'bleed onto the page,' as Hemingway would say. It's all for your reading enjoyment. Please enjoy the ride and thank you for placing your fingertips upon my freshly bared soul.

INTRODUCTION

With a new decade upon them, its infancy tumultuous and tension-filled, New Yorkers go about their day with their uniquely diverse purposes and still almost synchronized march toward it. PPE (personal protective equipment), hydroxychloroquine, and "flattening the curve" had not yet cycled into the colloquial lexicon and were still terms known almost exclusively to healthcare professionals and first responders. The decade had not yet come close to reaching a roar unless you count potentially roaring toward conflict with Iran or the roar from Republicans after the president, impeached in the House of Representatives, was resoundingly acquitted by the Senate. Yes, the 2020s were off to a rocky start and the country was longing—practically begging—for the real roaring prosperity and galvanizing jazz music of one hundred years ago. If the 2010s were definitively the all-digital, iPhone, Instagram, selfies R us era, the 2020s possessed the imagination for something much more substantive and still reminiscent of a bygone golden era.

But before the decade could use its first one hundred days as a runway for commercial and cultural propulsion, almost everything that everyone enjoyed and took for granted was forcibly removed by factors unforeseen and uninvited. There was about to be a "social distancing," not just of the populace, striving to optically measure and maintain six feet apart, but of citizen and trust in government, denizens, and view of foreigners.

These were strange times and growing stranger still and there was still an election looming that would be a referendum on the type of society that the American people desired to live in. The entire year, to that point, had played out like one extended Friday the thirteenth, and by the time June had arrived there were nefarious forces attempting to seize control of the narrative—and the city—in a way diametrically opposed to the conservation and ascension of a decade before. New York City was soon a metropolis on the ropes, and its residents reflected this in their desperate combinations, thrown in retreat, as they collectively gasped for precious and elusive life-saving air.

CHAPTER 1

The Bridge of Life

On an almost achingly beautiful morning, in early June of 2020, severely clear skies hovered over New York City together with an invisible nuisance that was crippling the cosmopolis in a manner not witnessed since the Great Depression. It did not matter to Jaxton Bello that a glorious fireball provided the seasonal warmth that caused his skin to glow precisely as his internal light dimmed. The sun assaulted the towers of the colossal George Washington Bridge, and Jaxton plodded along the pedestrian ramp. He carried no briefcase or real purpose, it appeared, and yet his purpose for being there was as all too real, albeit brief.

He wore a fading shirt that read, "Austin 3:16," and had a messenger bag with an important message inside slung across his chest. There was true resolution drawn on his brows. The sun's flames painted the blue-gray suspenders in resplendent gold and splintered through the sleepy suspension cables while warming the uncharacteristically calm deck. But Jaxton did not care about the architecture, and there was both life and lifelessness in the lines and lanes of the bridge's connection during this truth-determining morning. Jaxton had a water funeral planned, and the sight of diagonally floating helium balloons that read, "COVID-19 victims," did nothing but encourage him in his goal.

He squeezed the bridge railing with his trembling hand, and the bridge shook back as an oversized supermarket tractor-trailer rumbled across. It was as if this melancholy man was offering a proper goodbye to the majestic structure, both citizens of a city of disparity, their horizons erased after opportunities took their usual plunge. This would ring even truer as the pandemic ate its way through the once palatial city. Jaxton would presumably not live to see the recovery and reconstruction. His face wrinkled as pain applied its habitual folds. He believed it would all end on the riverside of the walkway that morning. He tossed a knee over the railing, clinging tightly to the palisade. He was troubled but, suddenly was in trouble with the off-duty NYPD sergeant who wagered that Jaxton would be there and crossed the bridge's span with the determination of a bullet. Cason Sax leapt over the jersey divider, moved toward Jaxton like a forest fire, and seized him violently. They stood on opposite sides as the proud polygons of the Manhattan skyline stood spectator-like. The two men grappled and tempted gravity. Jaxton hoped his journey would terminate 212 feet down into a liquid grave. There were no honks coming from the few commuter vehicles crossing the expanse and no howls as the wind had gone silent and two humans converged on one spot, ornamenting a bridge as it was not intended. The outcome of their dance would define the day and this very story.

The now almost indeterminable balloons carried their message of grief, and the morning carried the type of drama that mundane mornings rarely do. But this bridge was not a routine actor. It was 604 feet of towering destiny-deciding steel. The bridge's necklace lights were unlit, but all would be illuminated on this warming dawn. The bridge of life would decide the fate of the faithless Jaxton, fighting like a fugitive for the right to die amid New York City's morning stretch. Prior to this walk, he had asked himself the existential questions, "How much do you push forward? How much do you protect what lies behind?"

"Get the fuck off me!" Jaxton yelled, his shirt ripping slightly underneath his armpit.

"I can't let you do this,'" Cason replied, bear-hugging his friend and trying to summon a burst of strength to rip him back to the safe side.

"It's over," Jaxton proclaimed, wriggling in Cason's tensed arms.

Suddenly, Jaxton's feet left the ground, then he was hurtling pavement bound. He sailed through the air, and both men tumbled to the ground, rolling and striking their heads against a metal divider.

"That's fucked up, Cason!" Jaxton shouted at his friend. "I trusted you!"

"You're fucked up. You're gonna do this to Grace?"

"Don't fucking mention Grace," he warned as he let out an anguished cry.

"Yeah, I'm gonna mention her. She loves her daddy so much. You are her *world*. You want another man raising your daughter, Jax? You want another man walking her down the aisle?"

"Stop saying that!" Jaxton replied, lobbing punches at his pal.

"You're not gonna become another uncounted victim of this goddamn pandemic. You're coming with me, and I'm taking you to Presbyterian hospital," he stated, snatching his friend up by the neckline.

"I'm not going to the goddamn hospital."

"I wasn't asking."

"So, what . . . you're going to take me at gunpoint or something?" Jaxton asked between severely strained breaths. He threw himself on the deck.

"I'll do what is required," Cason answered, pulling out his silver Smith & Wesson 9mm service weapon. "Get up! Get up off the ground now. And take your messenger bag with you."

"Shoot me. I can't go back and face them now. Just fucking blast me!"

"I'm not blasting you. You are going home. You are going to face your wife and daughter, and you're going to turn this tragedy into a triumphant finish. Just like how you end all those articles you write, with hope and optimism and all that happy shit."

"There is no hope. The magazine is going out of business. It's all done because of COVID. I'm out of a job. I have failed. As a *man*, I have failed! I can't pay that mortgage anymore. I have nowhere and nothing to write about."

Cason was too determined to let Jaxton's obituary be written on this day.

"Oh yeah? Well, what if you could?" Cason asked.

"What the hell do you mean 'what if I could?'"

If you had one last article to write, what would you write about? If you could write about anything?"

"What?"

"You're an author. That's your gift. If you could write one last story, to leave a lasting impression on everybody in the world, what would you write about? What would you say?" Cason elaborated, growing increasingly frustrated.

"What kind of . . . Is this one of your hostage negotiation techniques?"

"This is not a technique. Just answer," he pressed.

Jaxton took a long pause and reflected on the question deeply. Tears were blotted on his crimsoned face.

"New York. I would write about New York City. Before it went to shit. When the magic still lived here. Even after 911 when lower Manhattan was eviscerated. When you could proudly display an American flag because you knew the country and the city were going to come back and rise like a phoenix from the ashes. I would write about the golden years, long before this terrible virus silenced the roar of the new '20s. Before this feckless mayor allowed the city to decay and become an unimpeded playground for the homeless and mentally ill. Seven straight years of deterioration leading to this. I used to love her. I used to be *in love* with her. Now I barely recognize her. Everybody is wearing masks, socially distancing, and falling into the depths of depression. It's like the city is collectively sick. Not just the people in it, but the metropolis itself. It's sick. New York is dying. Did you know what an N95 mask was in January? What about *contact tracing*? Did you ever think you'd see New Yorkers remain six feet apart from one another?"

"So you're going to fix the problem by jumping off your favorite landmark?" Cason interrupted. "How many times did we jog this bridge together, Jax? We trained for the half on this bridge. I have a picture in my living room of us showing off our medals."

"You know," Jaxton started, "I always saw myself as a microcosm of New York. As her fortunes went, so too did mine. I thought she would boom again in 2020. That boom was killed. Now we have masks stretched across our mouths to mute whatever shout of protest we might have mustered."

"You're yearning for the Roaring Twenties? That was a one-shot deal," Cason stated. "You have a wife and a daughter now. You have a beautiful family. We had our golden era. Look at all we achieved in the last ten years. Look at the friends we made. Look where life took us—Puerto Rico, Costa Rica, Australia, *Paris*! We lived a lifetime in a decade, Jax. We reached heights most people never climb to. But now you have a legacy you are building for them. Seeds planted ten years before sowed into the American Dream. You can't just destroy that."

It is certainly true that Jaxton Bello and Cason Sax had a memorable decade leading up to this ignominious convergence. For most of the epoch, they sort of roared all on their own, sometimes accompanied by a variety of unforgettable acquaintances.

The two men were similar but different. One battled life in a linear fashion, the other fought it, to a greater degree, in semicircles. But they both punched. After sparring so much that morning, the two men, from different industries and different walks of life, walked off that bridge and into the past after brushing up against death in a manner that left real scars. Staring Jaxton dead in his face was the prospect of returning home to a child barely three feet tall and gazing into intelligent brown eyes that viewed him as the world itself. He would wander and wonder if he could go home sweet home, feeling as sour and homeless as he felt in that fleeting transience into death. He would not return home immediately but, rather, venture inward into his consciousness, to his most cherished memories, haunting failures, and into a vivid and precarious remembrance of indelible things past. He would voyage through a New York City frozen by the pandemic and retrace his footsteps into the cordon of his favorite crime scenes. This is Jaxton Bello's soul-baring *odyssey*.

Chapter 2

A Decade of Prosperity

Ten years ago, Jaxton and Cason met at a throbbing nightclub on the West Side waterfront in Lower Manhattan as the summer and their careers heated up. Back then, Jaxton was the type of guy who enjoyed the sound of ice rattling at the bottom of a glass in dark corners of sweat-filled sex boxes. Cason was an NYPD sergeant who did not belong in the disreputable venue but was drawn to it at the request from Jaxton to interview him for a crime story. Jaxton would perform a subsequent ride-along later that month, after extensive socializing.

"Are you sure you want to see what I see on the mean streets?" Cason asked. "It's not Hollywood. This blood really stains."

"That's exactly what I want. I want to write about the raw, sordid side of things—shots fired in the projects, emotionally disturbed men with *machetes*, heroin addicts overdosing and collapsing facedown into the shattered glass that is a remnant of the disbanded broken-windows theory," Jaxton described.

"Wow. The public information officer told me you were good. I dig the colorful imagery. But you have to be careful," Cason warned. "It's one thing to write about it rhetorically. It's another thing to see it happen to real people. *That* stays with you for a long time."

On that night, as the beginning of a friendship forged under dim light and as the alcohol took hold, they both eyed an inebriated Adriana Topaz. She was the type of girl who could commit you with a hand wave. She was intimidatingly beautiful but carried the pain in her eyes of a traveler;

one that longs for a place to call home. She modeled chestnut-hued, ruler-straight hair and light almond-colored eyes. Her lips were the shape of a horizontal recurve hunting bow and her tongue was as sharp as the arrows it could fire at its targets. Adriana's soul breathed flames, but the picturesque water undulating along the West Side Highway, with the lights of New Jersey illuminating the expanse, provided her calm tonight. Jaxton was preparing to unsettle her in his unique mercurial way. He closed the distance, swaggering with confidence.

"What's your name?" Jaxton offered during the first eye contact.

"Not stale at all. Why don't you just go ahead and ask me if I shaved my honeypot tonight and cut out all the perfunctory conversation?" she asked before continuing, "I mean if you're going to be that uncreative?"

"Wow. What . . . candor. You, my dear, are unfairly beautiful. But I would never be so forward regarding your grooming habits of your erogenous area."

"Oh. A gentleman, I see," she replied sarcastically. "What a relic."

"Says the gentle*woman*, of course?"

"You look like someone with immaculate *um* . . . maintenance although that's none of my business. But I heard retro is in this summer," blabbered a tipsy Cason.

The three paused before erupting in laughter. They clinked tumblers as sultry jazz music seduced from the swank speakeasy, seemingly from behind the perpetual *clack* of ricocheting pool balls and fluffy conversations.

"Do you want to go for a drive?" Jaxton asked. "I have a deadline for an article tomorrow morning, and I need some inspiration. It's not my true crime article yet, so you have nothing to worry about. At least nothing that I can foreshadow."

"Absolutely not. I'll stay right here," Adriana responded. "Unless you're taking me to Tavern on the Green for caviar and filet mignon, I'm staying put. You and your boyfriend can go."

"His *husband*," Cason corrected.

"Congratulations on the nuptials," she replied.

"Thank you. But we have an open relationship."

"There's destiny out there tonight," Jaxton began. "And it involves you. I've lived an entire lifetime just inside my mind. I'm a deeply analytical overthinker. I've imagined every scenario possible, including this one," he rambled.

"What is this one?" she inquired.

"The one where you and I just go with the flow and say, 'Fuck it,'" he replied.

"The one where I say, 'Fuck it,'" she repeated, "or do I say, 'Fuck *off*?'"

Jaxton grabbed her hand, and she resisted at first but then decided to take a chance. He seemed like a walking fiesta and she seemed to just move her feet as he pulled her out the front door. Cason followed them hurriedly, chugging one last sip and slapping his drinking glass down on a cheap coaster on somebody else's table. On that night, he would mostly be a bodyguard. It did not seem to bother him. He was open-minded enough to let the momentum of the night carry him into tomorrow.

Cason was an island onto himself. He was toughened up in the bygone "We own the night" theater of the NYPD's yesteryear. It was a "take no prisoners" era where the bad guys were just that and treated accordingly. He viewed himself as a courier of justice, and as a supervisor in the NYPD, he had a front-row seat to the greatest show on Earth. And by his own accounting, it was a pure circus. Jaxton drove, and Adriana released her hair out of the front passenger window as Cason texted someone named Reyna and smiled mischievously in the rear passenger seat. They arrived at a gentlemen's club on Forty-Third Street and Eighth Avenue called Pumpkin Pies, and Cason immediately displayed his glimmering gold sergeant's badge to the bouncer, granting him and his acquaintances free admission.

"Like I told you guys back there: my job opens doors to the world," Cason bragged.

They entered and parted some beaded curtains, obtaining wristbands and proceeding to a throbbing seating area with an illuminated stage and ladies in various stages of undress.

"I've never been to a strip club before," Adriana divulged as she raised her voice above pulsating beats and catchy auto-tuned lyrics.

"There's really nothing to it," Jaxton explained. "It's a game, and the objective of it is to keep your money in your wallet."

"Why did you bring me here?" Adriana demanded as her head swiveled at everything orbiting around her.

"I wanted to see how you would react," Jaxton replied.

"Well, I'm reacting like this, confused," she answered. "Utterly."

"I like the champagne here," Jaxton declared. "It's actually sparkling wine from the Sonoma Valley, but that can be our little secret. It has a note of vanilla cake. It's creamy with just a hint of tart. A friend of Cason works in the bar, and he usually fills my flute up for free three or four times."

"So, you're a frequent flier at strip clubs?"

"No . . . I've only been here one other time," Jaxton responded.

"Right. So what are we waiting for?" she asked against hip-hop vibrations and a soaring R and B bridge. "Tell your friend to bring us three flutes full of that exquisite sparkly shit you're raving about."

The three consumed champagne and watched the exotic dancers carry the New York night on their tattooed backs.

"They spritz on fragrances throughout the night to mask the natural smell of woman," Cason crudely announced.

"I'm a woman. I think I can infer what goes on here hygienically," Adriana scolded. "And we should show some appreciation for their artistry and subjecting themselves to our objectification and your male gaze and give up some of our dollars to them. We already got admission and bubbly for free. The least we can do is compensate the dancers for their interpretation of these urban anthems."

"Yes, ma'am," Jaxton agreed, taking a few twenty-dollar bills out of his pocket.

At just that moment, a dancer going by the name Reyna squatted down next to Cason and massaged his knee.

"Hi, Papi. Welcome back. I didn't know it was going to be a foursome," she stated in a mild Dominican accent.

"Hey, Saxy. You guys get any media cases in Harlem lately?" Jaxton interrupted.

"C'mon, Jax, Harlem is up and coming. Gentrification. Aside from EDPs defecating in the streets on 125th Street and Lexington Avenue, everything is immaculate up there."

"Oh yeah. It's pristine up there, huh? I'm looking to rent a tent in front of one of the methadone clinics."

"I *said* I didn't properly prepare for a foursome. Who's the new girl?" Reyna pressed, plopping herself onto Cason's lap and depositing a vivid lipstick stain on his stubbly cheek.

"Thank you, baby," he responded. "We literally just met her. You know I only have eyes for you, baby. That's Jaxton's chick."

"Yeah right," Reyna replied, playfully slapping his face.

A second stripper, a long-legged Russian blonde, placed a frothy flute in Reyna's hand, and she abruptly clinked glasses with a distracted Cason.

This spilled his golden beverage as Reyna guzzled her drink lavishly. Adriana drew her face close to Jaxton's and invaded his mouth with a citrus-tinged kiss.

Currency fluttered through the air like a hundred little wayward kites, strobe lights cutting through them and revealing hypersexualized patrons' faces, buried in flesh. Jaxton and Adriana, inebriated by drink and the charismatic New York night, had commenced intimacy that would escalate well into the dawn. Cason would end up in a cluttered studio apartment on 168th Street, bringing the night to a climactic close for him and Reyna and postponing his interview with his enamored associate.

That entire scene felt light-years removed from the pair's despondent ride home from the bridge and through Washington Heights after Jaxton barely made it out of the first week of June of 2020 alive. It was strange for Jaxton to look out the window and see people in their vehicles, and the scarce pedestrians on the streets, donning surgical masks, counterfeit N95 masks, and homemade variations of assorted colors and patterns. Schools had been shut down for in-class learning. There was a class war waging between essential and nonessential employees and the politicization of masks that pitted wearers versus non-wearers. Nurses and doctors at city hospitals were receiving first-hand experience as to what it was like to triage in a war zone. And the once-thriving economic engine of New York City had been turned off deliberately—restaurants shut their doors and the lack of work turned many New Yorkers into avid day drinkers.

Jaxton considered his dramatically changed landscape and having to return home, harboring shame, arriving at the emotional valley after ten practically opulent years of steady professional ascent and personal growth. It would burn his soul to hear the word, "Dad-dy," mouthed cheerfully by a daughter, Grace, whose trust he betrayed by trying to thrust himself off Othmar Ammann's gargantuan structure. As the first great pandemic of the new '20s decimated the once-flourishing life in the city, Jaxton faltered as well. He previously had a highly romanticized view of the city, once writing at the conclusion of his weekly article:

> He did not know her in the way that he wanted to, but he knew her in a way that he could never forget. She was not so much holding the universe in place as much as she was holding their *place* in the universe. She was

the bookmark in a chapter that had not yet been written. "Once upon a time" waiting for the right time, the perfect moment. Perhaps it was a bridge too far. Perchance it was a staircase to nowhere. He was banking on it being a stairway to heaven. Beyond the fire and brimstone of his current trials, amidst the pain of fighting battles with heavyweight demons, she ethereally floated on the timeline of his consciousness as both destination and destiny in one celestial package. In his romantic imagination, her beauty prevailed as the one essence that shone through like the rays of first blush through flowy sheer linens. He marched into her, hoping she would be his greatest love of this life or the next. Her name was New York.

Jaxton wrote that piece at the pinnacle of his writing career that would see him pen a *New York Times* best-selling book, receive major writing awards, and author some truly encapsulating articles regarding New York City's endless recomposition and quest for glory. His columns had a massive following and his social media presence would expand exponentially with each new popularized site. Jaxton possessed the walk of a man who had paid his dues, learned the business and climbed to the top. He was the it writer in a changing New York literary landscape but with unspoken problems fermenting underneath the surface.

When his daughter was born, his entire perspective changed. He parented almost exclusively on instincts, more artist than scientist, often whisking his princess away to where she could eat ice cream with sprinkles or get a new doll. Once, he cried in an unlit corner of the Toys R Us parking lot in Yonkers with his daughter asleep in the car seat. Parenting was something that inspired and beguiled him all in the same motion.

He wanted to achieve better for his family but had a thirst for the boundless freedom and access that being a popular writer in New York City afforded him. He purchased a house in Westchester to deliver what he felt was his obligation, the American Dream.

While Jaxton was exploring the manufactured beauty of New York, Cason was toiling in its congenital destitution. He went from the crack-controlled, cop-patrolled foot posts of forgotten South Bronx corners to gentrified avenues in Harlem's galvanized hubs during the cultural and urban renewal. He was promoted to sergeant special assignment mid-decade and used his gold badge as a diamond key to unlock the city's greatest monuments and trendiest tourist trampolines. He and Jaxton would bounce from the Empire State Building to the top of Rockefeller Center on the same afternoon with a beautiful female companion each before Cason reported to the precinct to work the ghoul shift. Operation Impact was still going on in crime-prone neighborhoods, post stop and frisk, and Cason was then in charge of guiding his young recruits through a hyper-scrutinized profession. Jaxton would occasionally partner on the ride-along, discussed during the duo's first summit, and was taken aback by how a massively neglected population languished in New York's urchin shell. Jaxton once composed a piece focusing on his pal after accompanying him on four brutal hours in the Melrose section of the Bronx and wrote insightfully about him:

> He wanted to return to halcyon mornings before shots were fired, before unsteady foot pursuits through needle-laden project courtyards. Before puddles of rain, gasoline, and blood held a reflection for fallen angels, facedown, pulseless, and earth-less now. He longed for the un-decimated parts of the city where commerce and cash covered up social injustices and disparity, where Broadway show marquees provided a Playbill path to fizzy chardonnay and feigned opulence. But he was a public servant, and he served a forgotten community. Each day he walks, chest out, into its eye, knowing resentment toward him is deep-rooted, and bullets are intended for him and those of his ilk. But he smiles and empathizes and still cares. Despite the daily diet of spilled shell casings, he is somehow inoculated from desensitization.

The deeper Cason got into his NYPD career, the more inelegantly he saw New York City age. Jaxton recorded this very trajectory in the pages of his avant-garde publication, *Metropolis Adjacent*. He had a stately office in the Chrysler Building, and every day, he stepped into the lobby's art deco stylings, replete with its imported marble, bronze handrails, and granite walls.

"Good morning, Mr. Bello!" the enthusiastic doorman saluted from behind a newspaper.

As he rode the rich wood-paneled elevators up to his office, he thought about the eagle-headed gargoyles piercing out into the city and ornamenting the imperial structure. He would ponder on how they had witnessed the evolution of the city, and he used it to fuel his writings. When his daughter turned one, he took her to work and held her atop one of the eagles on the sixty-first floor. He prompted her to close her eyes, and they imagined themselves to be the birds of prey, taking flight over the fabulous city as it rose during the machine age of the 1920s.

"Show me how you fly, baby," he instructed. "Let's spread our wings and see New York the way the birds do. You're ready to fly, my love?"

He made a whooshing sound as he guided her compact body, holding her firmly and keeping her tiny frame securely pressed up against him. The air hit them just the right way to make them feel unrestricted. Almost in earnest, eyes shut in excitement, they soared. He included Grace in his column that week, intertwining the evolving city with his growing toddler and delivering this reflection:

> The moments are tender, and they evaporate quickly, and then you are that age no more. It is strange to think that a day spent at work, away from you, is a significant portion of your life right now. You are young, but not as young as you used to be. I am used to you needing me and your mother for everything, but now there are things you no longer require us for. Your eyelashes are longer than any woman's I know, and your mole is the envy of every girl not named Cindy Crawford. I envy your tenacity; you simply *must* connect that highchair seat belt yourself and hear the satisfying *click*. You are the air in our home. I have woken up every night, exhausted or drunk, and stumbled to your crib just to listen to the sound of your breaths. Amidst the darkness of night, we are the only two people in the world. I have loved you since you were affirmed by a blue line on a home pregnancy test. Your mother's tears that day were the sincerest thing I have ever seen or tasted. I have carried you every single day of your life and held you like sweet life itself. Because you are sweet life itself. To me. As I sit here writing about you. Love, Dad-dy who is smitten over his amazing Grace."

When he wrote that article back in 2018, he walked over to the high-rise's competitor, the Empire State Building, where Cason was positioned in front. Cason was visiting and inspecting two rookie officers on their foot post.

"Can I get a scratch too, Sergeant Sax?" Jaxton mocked.

"I should be asking for your autograph, Mr. famous best seller," Cason teased.

"Well, you know, I couldn't have done it without you. I had to see the poverty you saw to appreciate the abundance and luxuriousness I write about."

"Okay, guys, you're good," Cason assured the officers. "Go ahead up to the observation deck on the eighty-sixth floor. Enjoy the sights. If the lieutenant comes around, I'll tell him you're checking for King Kong."

The cops were swept in by the revolving doors, into the grand art deco atrium.

"King Kong, huh?"

"I don't know why I said that . . . Hey, do you know who I ran into today?" Cason asked.

"King Kong?"

"No. Adriana Topaz," Cason revealed.

"Adriana Topaz . . . from our bachelor days?"

"Come on, man. Stop playing dumb. There's only one Adriana Topaz in the world! She gave me her phone number for you."

"I still have her phone number," Jaxton replied.

"She said it's a new number, a 929-area code," Cason clarified. "I guess she had a problem with some guy stalking her."

"Well, that wasn't me, obviously," Jaxton informed.

"It *should have* been," Cason asserted. "You almost proposed to her, right?"

"Um . . . I uh . . . I went to Forty-Seventh Street, inquiring about rings," Jaxton admitted.

"The diamond district?" Cason chastised. "The grand larceny unit makes a lot of collars down there. Place is a bona fide shithole."

"It's more of an anachronism, like an ancient market," Jaxton explained. "One of the diamantaires was holding a special pear-shaped stone for me. Then he absconded back to Tel Aviv, so . . . things kind of just unraveled from there."

"Absconded? Anachron-chronism . . . whatever the fuck. Save your big words for your articles. Point blank, you loved that girl enough to look into rings for her."

"Either way, it wasn't meant to be. And then I met Waverly," Jaxton reminded.

"Waverly. She changed the entire game for you. But, damn, Adriana was almost the one."

"Almost . . ." Jaxton qualified before dreamily repeating, "*almost.*"

A few weeks after their strip club venture, Jaxton Bello and Adriana Topaz walked into the extravagant piazza at Lincoln Center for the Performing Arts, and her jade dress contained so much tulle bunched up underneath it that she could have used some train bearers to hold it up. The two deposited wishes attached to dull dimes into the magnificent dancing water fountains and walked into the atrium of the main hall like a benefactor and benefactress. There was a lava-red carpet that was Oscar-worthy and an absurdly opulent chandelier and two cascading staircases that led to a landing filled with champagne towers. The flutes were poured to the brim.

"You really know how to impress a gal," Adriana said, flirting with her uncanny eyes.

"So, you're saying you're impressed?" Jaxton verified as he extracted two chilly flutes from the counter.

"I'm saying you possess the know-how . . . the knowledge to impress a female human being," she qualified.

"Oh, that's—"

"Not, not necessarily this particular—"

"Oh stop," Jaxton responded.

"*This* female is not necessarily impressed yet," countered Adriana. "The first date was a titty bar. This is an opera hall. So we kind of have to average the two out and use the median."

"Maybe after the performance you'll be impressed."

"Maybe I will . . . and maybe I won't," she equivocated. "It depends what performance you're talking about."

Two hours later, Adriana was crying in her seat after the heart-breaking tragedy of *Swan Lake* ripped emotion out of her perfectly mascaraed eyes. Jaxton admired her barely illuminated face and believed the tears to be the result of not just the power of ballet but of a deeper void of love existing within her. After the production, they flagged down a yellow taxicab and headed southbound from Broadway for the Mandarin Oriental Hotel in the spectacularly rebuilt Columbus Circle. Jaxton admired her walk, luminary-like, and anticipated a passionate evening overlooking Central Park.

"The ballet moved you, huh?" he probed upon arriving at their lavish hotel room.

"It spoke to my soul. The pain, the torment. Tchaikovsky must have really been on something when he wrote that score," Adriana opined. "It really affected me tonight."

"Pain is a universal language," Jaxton replied. "Whether its *Swan Lake*, *The Phantom of the Opera*, the New York Knicks . . . It's something everyone can identify—"

"The New York Knicks?" she questioned with a laugh.

"Yeah. I would argue that Patrick Ewing is as tragic a character as *The Swan Princess* or *The Phantom of the Opera* and markedly more talented than both."

"He's way more New York, I'll give you that," she replied, shooting an imaginary jump shot.

"It's true. This is the center of the universe. He played center for the Knicks. He was at the mathematical center of existence," Jaxton continued. "And he never won a championship despite his immense talents. That's tragic."

"Well, we all kind of have a little tragedy in us."

"What's your tragedy?" he inquired clumsily.

"If you're trying to get any tonight, you don't want to open up that Pandora's box." She dropped her cardigan to the floor, revealing an elegant toned back. "Just look at Fifty-Ninth Street. Central Park looks like a magic carpet from here. Absolutely breathtaking."

"The view is absolutely breathtaking from back here too."

The two came together like heavenly bodies and tasted each other's mouths as the Christopher Columbus statue appeared to gaze up at them. They climbed into a bed grand enough to fit four, and Jaxton entered her for the first time. Being inside her felt like home and like everything he had been searching for. He would long create these hyperbolic quests for a so-called goddess divine, and he thought he might have found her in the unforgettable Adriana Topaz.

After their climax, Jaxton and she drank from gold-rimmed champagne flutes, their naked silhouettes encased by the window frame and backlighted by the outward illumination from the then bustling city.

One entire bottle of Veuve Clicquot later, Jaxton slept, and his feminine lover lay awake in bed, crying like a fatherless child. Jaxton would have multiple roles to play if he were to become something more than a Saturday night Central Park South rendezvous to her. There were emotional layers to peel through, not just layers of lingerie, and Jaxton would be tested by her and her complicated past. But that night would have multiple rounds, and he inhaled the sugared scent hovering off her soft skin and silky hair. He put his lips to her warm vulva and guided her flavor into his awakened taste buds. He paused to take in the moment of consuming her innermost parts, swallowing when he could to savor what her body produced in response to him. They enjoyed one another while New York provided the canvas and the saturated color evocative of the most sensual Renoir.

But it was so far removed from that impressionistic night then. Time and destiny had moved Jaxton in a surprisingly different direction.

"I'll see if I give her a ring," Jaxton acquiesced.

"Poor choice of words."

"A buzz, a call! You know what I mean, asshole."

"I don't care if you do or if you don't. I'm just the messenger. She asked me to do it. But I'm team Waverly because . . . I really don't want to see my best friend get castrated in his sleep," Cason remarked, pantomiming scissors in his hand.

"Yeah, so funny. I kind of need my . . . you know. I'd like to try for a boy at some point."

"You can't build a dynasty without a boy," Cason remarked.

"I know. I need that boy. I love my girl though," Jaxton announced. "Both of them."

CHAPTER 3

Waverly Larkin Bello

In comparing romance to a flower once, Jaxton cautioned, "Love unfurls like a rose, but if you've ever bought a rose, you know what roses do." He, at times, wrote about what it was like to attempt to forge meaningful relationships in an illusory and impersonal city. Writing was his way of examining life in the city and the human condition at large. This informed his works and fed his obsessive drive to be the best at his craft and become a quintessential voice in the famed New York literary canon. He once revealed, with fire, during a New York One television interview:

> I want to capture New York as F. Scott did, the vitality, the promise, the celebratory spirit of achievement and high living, but also the greed. I want to capture it as J.D. Salinger did, the city as a stage or a sad playground for the anxious and how, amidst a large and busy city, one can feel so alone. I want to capture it as Toni Morrison did in *Jazz* with the way the 1920s roared differently in Harlem, the disparity, compared to other parts of the city, cavernous. There is electricity and hope in New York, but it can defeat and humble you just as quickly as it can lift you up into its peaks and sun-warmed spires.

That quote starkly contrasted to his very last article in *Metropolis Adjacent*, the column he penned before heading to the bridge, which he folded up and placed inside his messenger bag to help explain his actions if found. In that essay, he asked hypothetically,

> Where have all the beautiful people of New York City gone? Disappeared and making way for beautifully essential ones on the frontlines, not of entertainment, retail, and advertising but of health care, law enforcement, and food delivery. All of them veil their New York-ness with a potpourri of different face coverings, so they can remain healthy and revive the dying city. Manhattan is a ghost town where the most bustling haunts once existed. The Great White Way, where signage once dazzled and performances razzle-dazzled, is unilluminated. And in Harlem, where jazz frazzled American culture with its improvisation and syncopation, there is no music, no dance, and virtually no celebration. Times Square is bare, Columbus Circle, undiscovered and uninhabited. There is no contact to trace. Can you think of any other time like this? Educators teaching remotely, tape on supermarket floors to keep people six feet apart. No baseball, no basketball, no boxing. We went from zooming back and forth to zooming in front of a computer for hollow meetings. Handshakes, hugs, and kisses are detrimental to health, releasing criminals from jails, somehow advantageous. The only house where you can worship is your own, and we went from teaching toddlers the ABCs to teaching them about PPE. Conversation is minimized, hands are sanitized, and alcohol is gold whether rubbing or for drinking. I am drunk on despair and disdain for this virus and pleading with the pain of this process to depart. The virus has gone viral. In the media, on the web, and in the mesh of our society. The lattice is fraying, skies are graying, and all of New York is in permanent descent.

Those would be the writer's final words to the world if he never penned another article. And it was his flair for composition that allowed him to steal the heart of his dear wife, Waverly.

Jaxton Bello loved his wife with blood pumping passion. She tamed him and put an end to late-night gallivanting through New York's cityscape, and the notion that he was the essayist version of Derek Jeter. Jaxton was faithful and loyal to his wife but enchanted by the "what might have been" had he kept his bachelor status as his ascent as the most popular writer in New York commenced.

On the day of their first encounter, he fidgeted in a Riverdale barber's chair and visualized the future, their future. He had purchased sapphire-blue Cole Haan shoes to step into his destiny, and a fragrance to match the excitement and energy of that hot summer night. She was serving drinks at a sports bar close to Yankee Stadium, and he was game to finally solidify his future with a partner to strut through life with. He arrived eager but was promptly rejected by the bouncer.

"You're not on the guest list, dude," uttered a grotesquely muscled man.

"Um . . . yeah. I have the e-mail confirmation right here," replied the much smaller Jaxton. "It says just show it to—"

"If you're not on my list, you can't get in. That's it. No exceptions," he reiterated.

"I have to get in tonight. Waverly invited me personally. Do you know Waverly? Miss Larkin? She's . . ."

And in that instant, an ivory-skinned Puerto Rican enchantress of two and a half decades descended from a seemingly invisible staircase. She wore a diminutive black dress, black heels, and sanguine lipstick. Her hair was pulled back tightly in a high ponytail, accentuating her upturned caramel-brown eyes. Her smile, razor-sharp at the corners, opened a portal for him. The entire introduction felt like a slow-motion reveal of a movie money shot. Jaxton, however, was no spectator but, rather, an aviator. Piloting his life in a new direction after scorching all social aspects of the earth across half a decade of polygamy and ethically conscious debauchery.

"Hello," he mustered, unsurely extending his wrist for a handshake.

"Hi there," she greeted, bypassing his outstretched arm for a kiss that would bring them cheek to cheek within seconds of their initial engagement. "Pleasure to finally meet you. I mean, the e-mails were so beautiful. You have such a way with words. But I wanted to make sure there was a real person behind all that the poetry."

"Oh, I'm a real person," he affirmed, uncomfortable still. "I'm a person and a poet."

"Of course, you are."

His already extended arm naturally went to the midpoint of her back and slid down to the slope just above her amply protruding buttocks. Her svelte arm went reflexively across his opposite shoulder, and they sustained the embrace for just a second longer than is customary. Their fragrances blended, and their eyes glimmered nervously, and she escorted him up to the seating area on the vibrant second floor.

"Wow. It is nice in here," he stated generically, looking around for some adjectives that he might infuse into his speech.

"It's not bad," she countered honestly. "I'm actually looking forward to getting out of here, out of this dress, and going someplace less . . . sweaty." She finished her sentence with a giggle and offered to take his blazer.

"Oh, so you want to go someplace else?" he inquired, still a step slow.

"Of course!" she exclaimed. "How else are we going to get to know each other?"

Jaxton smiled, his confidence slowly returning. He looked down at the sapphire of his shoes and removed his wool blazer, a tell-tale symbol of severe overdress. His V-neck shirt revealed the musculature of his upper chest, which caught Waverly's eye, and his biceps were adequately framed by his short sleeves. He looked at his timepiece as if it would advance the time forward to when they could be alone and could commence the rest of their lives together.

"I'll be right back. Just let me get rid of these drinks," she whispered alluringly.

Despite the magic that floated over their initial meeting, and their roaring liftoff into engagement, marriage, and parenthood, it could be argued that the figurative wave crest of his life was experienced during his time with Adriana. Jaxton remembered this well, and as he considered acting on Cason's message, he prepared himself for a phone call that could plunge him back into an ostensibly finalized era. When Jaxton was at that crossroad, he contemplated going back.

After the bridge, Jaxton was at yet another junction. But he needed to move forward. Forward meant going home. And home was not easy. The saying *"You can't go home again,"* was starting to weigh on Jaxton as he stalled after leaving the bridge. There really is no place like home, but home can only be home, unadulterated, at one point in time. The individual is not the same person, compositionally, once they depart, and Jaxton was certainly no longer the person who he was when he walked out the front door that morning.

Jaxton feared going home in the afternoon of his attempted suicide because it would undo all that he had built over the course of half a decade. He did not want his family to see him in such a compromised state. He would have to confront and resolve the question, "How much do you push forward? How much do you preserve what lies behind?" as there was nowhere left to hide. Or so it seemed. Getting off that bridge and renewing his zest for life was the equivalent of pushing forward. But it would undo the body of work, the reputation, and the image that he had carefully crafted over the course of his physical and intellectual prime. To have leapt off that structure was to preserve his achievements like when a promising artist dies young. He would not decline in the public eye, his image would remain impeccable and preserved forever. But was getting off that bridge fighting back? Or was Jaxton coming home to gradually decay and see his greatness fade in the eyes of his family? Would it, in fact, tarnish everything that preceded it? These were coliseum-sized questions for the pugilistic Jaxton to answer as he had to notify fate whether he sought to return home *with* his shield or *on* it.

Jaxton decided he would not immediately return to Westchester, to the picturesque sky-blue home he purchased by the sweat of his brow and his writing acumen to look a doe-eyed three-year-old juror in her eye. It was easier to take a cab to Times Square, the betrayed and cast-off epicenter of New York, and revisit the unchangeable past.

Once he arrived at Fifty-First Street, Jaxton made his way to the Gershwin Theatre. He snuck in through an unsecured door and gently walked through the mesmerizing rotunda. He took a seat in the last row of the rear mezzanine and gazed out at the 1,900 empty seats facing the arc of the stage. A map of *The Land of Oz* still hung above the unoccupied platform, a literal sleeping dragon hovering ominously above that. There was still a small stack of playbills in the aisle. He looked at the image of the two witches on the cover, and he reminisced on that first date at that very venue with Waverly. It was billed with anticipation as Wicked Friday, and on that night, they both enhanced their looks, their charm, and their expectations for the future under the yellow marquee bulbs of the eponymous theater.

"You look like a goddess divine, no hyperbole," Jaxton praised.

"You look like . . ." she scanned around for nouns floating in the air, "like an Adonis! As a matter of fact, you should tell people that is your name tonight."

"You look like an Adonia, and Aphrodite and every other Greek goddess that ever graced the planet."

They embraced and walked toward the concession stands where he ordered large souvenir sippy cups of sparkling wine.

"This is ambrosia we're drinking," he stated with a smile. "Do you know what F. Scott Fitzgerald said about champagne?"

"'Too much of anything is bad, but too much champagne is just right'?"

"He did say that didn't he?" Jaxton agreed. "But I was thinking, 'Among the whisperings and the champagne and the stars.'"

"That works too. Tonight, we are the stars. Tonight, we can be whatever we want. We can be Gatsby and Daisy if that's who you love."

"I do love them but . . . didn't they both die?"

"Daisy didn't die. Myrtle did!" she corrected.

"Myrtle? Okay, so we can be F. Scott and Zelda," he countered.

"Well, they actually died!" she noted before letting out a giddy laugh.

"Oh, right. Yeah, they did die. Everybody dies. But at least they were married. Sure, their marriage was tumultuous. Sure, he was an alcoholic and she was crazy, but that's life sometimes."

"So you want the marriage part or the crazy part? You decide. Because I'll be crazy for you tonight if you can handle that."

"Shit. I'm halfway to alcoholism. You might as well be crazy," he said, downing the bubbly in his souvenir cup with abandon.

She took a large sip from hers too, and they kissed deeply as theatergoers avoided them to place their overpriced orders. They embraced as if wanting to permeate each other before moving toward their aisle. He scooped her up, snatched a playbill with the free hand, and deposited her somewhere in the vicinity of their row. Bubbly spilled on her shoulder, and he tasted it off her skin. Some trickled down her black dress and it was as if they themselves were spilling all over each other in their undersized seats. They twisted together and shared champagne-infused kisses while pocketbooks and playbills fell under the cushions of their assigned marks. A Broadway show was never so physical and exciting for two of its spectators.

When the character, Elphaba, belted, "And nobody, in all of Oz. No Wizard that there is or was, is ever gonna bring me down!" Waverly sang along with the actress. She pantomimed and emoted, and Jaxton simply began to fall for her. During the intermission, more liquid gold was purchased and splashed. It was as if life itself was about to be drenched in champagne and enter a stage of perpetual celebration.

That night, the mystique and aura of Times Square floated them toward the Marriot Marquis and a hotel room in the sky overlooking the iconic tourist attraction. Illuminated Coca-Cola advertisements; giant golden arches; a *Phantom* mask; and a red rose; and an image of a big, shiny apple inundated their sense of sight. They stared out at the city of the future with their future looking like an edifice that would burgeon and rise within it. They held each other and fell sideways onto a bed seemingly the size of half a basketball court. They did not consummate that night; there would be much time for that. But they slept in each other's arms and connected on a spiritual level that was an investment intended to pay dividends later. They had the rest of their lives for that, or at least that was their wager.

Currently, in a vastly different place in life, a despondent Jaxton picked a *Wicked* playbill up off the step, rolled it up, and placed it in his back pocket. He failed to leave with one on that indelible night with Waverly.

"Hey! Are you the cleaner?" someone of authority at the Gershwin Theater yelled.

"Am I the cleaner?" Jaxton parroted. "No. Why would I be the cleaner?"

"Then get the hell out of here! We're still under quarantine. Who let you in?"

Jaxton speedily bolted for the front door. He stutter-stepped in front of a meticulously arranged souvenir table, undisturbed since New York City was put on hold, still displaying ostentatious prices. He lobbed a twenty-dollar bill toward the table and stuffed a small *Wicked* snow globe into the cushioned compartment of the messenger bag that adorned his shoulder. He evaded the theatre manager and zipped past the sign reading 222 W. Fifty-First Street and into *The Great White Way*. Times Square was surreally and numbly unpopulated, and it was as if he was running through a Hollywood set. He made his way westbound on Fifty-First street, a flash running past gaudy LED lights, toward the Museum of Modern Art.

Jaxton caught his breath on Sixth Avenue. He looked at the LED screen on his phone, whose background was a picture of Grace, that was virtually glowing. He looked at her big brown eyes beaming with life, curiosity, and wonder for the world. Her thin lips curved up in a heart-warming smile. It was as if the future was reaching back to the present.

The image transfixed him, and he stood on Fifty-Third Street and Sixth Avenue, crying. The crying rose from a sob to an ugly sob and then to an outright wail. There was no other human on the Avenue of the Americas to offer so much as a tissue to him or even just to stop and stare. Cason was not there to prop him back up; his only company was thoughts, which drifted. As lonely as he was, his mind wandered to Adriana. Then his phone abruptly rang.

"Hello," he said through sniffles.

"Are you back home yet?" Cason asked in a scolding tone.

"Home? No, man, I uh . . . I decided I had to pick something up in the city," Jaxton mumbled.

Cason erupted. "Pick something up in the city? The city is closed, man! You promised me you were going to take your ass back home. Waverly and Grace are waiting for you."

"No, they're not."

"What do you mean, 'No, they're not'?"

"They aren't waiting for me. I told Wave I was going to do some research for my next book. They're not expecting me right now."

"Okay. Listen, Jax. Maybe they aren't waiting by the door for you, but after what you almost did this morning, they are waiting for you to return home and restart your life with them. I am certain of this," Cason emphasized.

"I'm not ready for that yet," he countered.

"Well, you better get ready! I am a sergeant in the SRG unit. That's the strategic response group. We are citywide. We will strategically respond and snatch your ass up! You need to tell me what street you're on because I'm about to deploy my entire platoon down there to find you. I'm sending an RMP to you right away. Now, where the hell are you, Jax?"

"Cason, I know you care about me, and I love you, brother. I swear that I do. You pulled me off that bridge. Only you could have done that. And I have questions about how you even knew that I going to—"

"Hey, once you're safe at home, I'll answer any question you want. I need you to return to your residence first like right now."

"I can't go home right this minute. I can't let them see me like this. I'm not ready to face Gracie yet. Imagine her seeing her father as a shell of himself."

"Listen to me. I understand your torment. Maybe not fully, but I can try and put myself in your shoes. I'm trying to empathize. But you were hanging off the fucking G. W. Bridge when I found you this morning, and that's not normal. I need to know that you are well and no longer suicid—"

"Hey! Cason. . . Sergeant Sax," he interjected.

"What? What is it, Jaxton?"

"Do you know if the sky is going to be clear tonight?"

"Do I know if the sky is going to be? I don't know. I'm not a meteorologist. I'm just a cop. There isn't a cloud in the sky right now. But cease with the bullshit. I need to know your location. Now, where are you?"

"For my part, I know nothing with any certainty, but the sight of the stars makes me dream," Jaxton recited.

He hung up his phone and approached the vestibule to the Museum of Modern Art, the preeminent center for contemporary art in the city. It was a venue that he happily ventured to many times before. But the feeling, the ambiance, the vibrations were vastly different on this momentous sun-kissed day than ever before. And Jaxton was determined to commence a reconciliation with the newly unsealed past in a way that would steer his actions like an artist guiding his paintbrush across a surrealist landscape.

CHAPTER 4

Unstarry Nights

At the MOMA, delivery of a large parcel was taking place precisely as Jaxton loitered by the impressive vestibule. He swiftly assisted one of the transporters with a larger, heavier item.

"Thank you, man," the carrier greeted.

"Yeah, no problem. I got you," Jaxton replied.

"You work at the museum?"

"Yeah, I'm one of the—I'm one of the . . . curators here."

"So, you know where this one goes? I think it's a Munch."

"Yeah. Just leave it with the guard."

"Excuse me! You have to sign in," a uniformed security guard yelled at the delivery man.

Jaxton slid past the guard, whose head was lowered while he reviewed the invoice. He strode into the central atrium. It was awe-inspiring to be alone in the museum, absent of any other art lovers, while the natural light entering through the atrium's skylight provided a type of haze that made the entire experience dreamlike. He ambled into the sculpture garden, past *Pair of Rocks*, and into the architectural oasis. The courtyard was his and only his, and he took in the garden landscape as never before. Jaxton meditated there, eyed a despondent-looking Matisse sculpture, and mimicked its sunken posture. He reflected on the events of earlier that day and imagined the outcome if Cason had not been so quick to act. Would the world look any different without him in it? he wondered. He contemplated for a while, pondering which direction he would steer his life. After the respite, he reentered the museum and made his way past a blinking chandelier to the second-floor chamber.

Jaxton ignored the fourth-floor gallery devoted to pop art, except for *Gold Marilyn Monroe*, and made a beeline for Vincent van Gogh's *Starry Night*. He had been exiled from his publication, *Metropolis Adjacent*, but he was perpetually chasing artists like the Dutchman. He had a dedication to his craft that was Van Gogh-like, Michael Jordan-esque, and as he himself conveyed, in the mold of the legendary F. Scott Fitzgerald. Jaxton slowly approached the 1889 masterpiece and stopped, coincidentally, six feet from it. He did not have to socially distance himself from anyone, but it was as if there was a force field around the canvas of the French village. He had always taken umbrage to a gold frame encasing a work that flawless.

"It's still perfect. It's still absolutely perfect," he whispered.

Jaxton gradually inched closer to the masterpiece and traced in the air the curves, swirling lines, flamelike cypress trees, and church spire of the work. He touched the thickly layered oil brushstrokes, setting off an alarm. He pulled the blue night sky, dotted with yellow stars, right off the museum wall. He held the painting in his hands like a mother holding a newborn child. Jaxton lied on the floor, raising and backlighting the painting against the skylight, and then wrapped his arms around it again.

At that moment, guards stomped toward the gallery, and Jaxton rose, crookedly hanging the painting back on the wall. He fled the opposite way, past some Picassos, and down the unelectrified escalator. An announcement blared over the public address system regarding an intruder stealing artwork. Jaxton ran into the souvenir shop, grabbed a flat *Starry Night* Christmas ornament, and flung a twenty-dollar bill out of his pocket onto the cashier's counter. He tucked the memento into the padded pocket of his messenger bag and zipped it up. Enclosing police sirens sounded closer to the museum now, and Jaxton scuttled past counterterrorism officers carrying long semiautomatic rifles.

"Someone is trying to steal *Starry Night*! It's a Dutchman with a beard and one ear," he quipped, pointing toward the entrance before his cellphone rang.

"What's up, Sarge?" he greeted, as his breathing intensified.

"I called a level 1 mobilization for you. I'm pulling up at the museum now. Stay there!" Cason ordered.

"How did you know I would be there?"

"The Van Gogh quote," Cason replied.

"I didn't take you for much of a fan of 'the little painter fellow.'"

"I'm not. Google, jackass."

"Jackass gotta go," Jaxton replied as he ran westbound on Fifty-Third Street, making a sudden right on Seventh Avenue toward Columbus Circle. The gorgeous green of Central Park guided his route as it peeked out from behind vacant buildings.

"You better stop running from me," Cason ordered.

"I told you I just need more time!"

"You're out of time, Jax! I have you as a suicidal EDP, which makes you a special category missing."

"The hell is that supposed to mean to the layperson?" Jaxton asked, huffing noticeably.

"It means I have a helicopter in the air that came all the way from Floyd Bennet Field in Brooklyn to locate you, my friend."

Jaxton could hear the rotor blades being whirled by the rotor mast. It was a thunderous, almost violent sound, and the aircraft cast a large shadow over Seventh Avenue.

"Is this my ride?" Jaxton gazed up in amazement at the landing skids of the blue-and-white whirlybird as he tucked himself into the B, D, and E line subway station.

"It's there to help find you and bring you to safety."

"Phone's about to cut off. You're gonna need a submarine," he scoffed, swiping his MetroCard and heading underground, motoring past a colony of transients in various states of repose and organized squalor.

The phone call concluded, and Jaxton stole a moment to admire the colorful mosaic adorning the tunnel wall, once representative of New York as a patchwork; never static, ever-changing, but now dormant.

The once vast and endless army of New Yorkers who utilized that station were now quartered, hunkered, quarantined, hidden, and dematerialized like embers in the wind around a garbage can bonfire. He crept to the end of the platform, and an E train bullied its way into the station. Jaxton entered the railroad car into a congress of vagabonds and disappeared with the piles of newspaper and a few tempest-tossed NYC essential workers in face masks.

"Next stop, Columbus Circle," the conductor announced soothingly.

The train rocketed north, and Jaxton was on his way to Columbus Circle to revisit the past and settle scores with bygone ghosts.

Jaxton rose from the tunnels, spangled in sweat, into the world-famous traffic circle on Fifty-Ninth Street. The voice of the city was still audible even amid the hushed sidewalks and silenced intersections. He stared up at the Christopher Columbus statue that had once peered into his room at the Mandarin Oriental. He could see both the Theater District and Lincoln Square from where he stood, memories of both pristine in his mind. He spotted a sign that read, "The Shops at Columbus Circle Time Warner Center," and engaged a security officer in a red jacket standing guard.

"I'm sorry, sir. We're closed to visitors," the gentlemen informed.

"I'm not a visitor, I'm here to be a guest on a CNN show."

"Sir, because of the pandemic, they're not taping the shows here right now," the guard answered.

"I know. I'm here to pick up the technical equipment to take home to do the interview from there," he improvised. "Mr. Vanderbilt is having me on tonight. I'm the writer, Jaxton Bello from *Metropolis Adjacent*. I write about New York."

"Yeah, that's right," the old man agreed. "You use all those big words, right?"

"No no," Jaxton remarked with a laugh, "not big words, sesquipedalian ones."

"Sesqui—who? Come on, Jack. You're making my brain hurt. The escalators are right behind me."

Jaxton approached the bald, rotund, nude statue of Adam guarding the north escalator of the shops. It was twelve feet of smooth bronze except for its penis, which was shiny and gold from tourists fondling him during photo-op stops. Jaxton paused for his own selfie with the giant sculpture, right then feeling very much like the first man himself. While the statue appeared plump and overfed, Jaxton began to feel hungry. He also needed a bathroom break, and so he sought out the facilities, which were located one floor above. He entered the lavatory and squeezed himself into a stall.

"Hello?" Jaxton replied to his vibrating phone.

"I hear an echo, so you must be on the shitter," Cason inferred.

"You have a keen ear, Sergeant. But . . . you know, you never called me this much when we were tearing up the New York nightlife."

"When we were tearing up the New York nightlife, I didn't find you dangling off the side of a bridge attempting to bungee jump without the cord. Now, where the hell are you? Are you back at the magazine?"

"The magazine canned me, remember? They're folding. I'm canceled. I'm somewhere utilizing the exquisite lavatorial facilities. I'm considering writing a review. But I can't give you a subliminal quote because, apparently, you belong on *Jeopardy.*"

"I told you, Google. C'mon Jax. Tell me where you are so I can meet you. You at MSG? Union Square? St. Patrick's Cathedral?"

"St. Patrick's Cathedral? Divine intervention just might be what I need right now. You found me once though. You can find me again, no?" Jaxton challenged.

"Jax, one of the questions on a special category missing report is 'Do you want media attention?' If I answer yes, we blast this out to all the outlets, and your family is going to find out. You might as well turn yourself in."

"Just answer no to the question, Case. Wait. Did you say, 'Turn yourself in?'" he asked. "I'm not wanted for anything, am I? What! Am I suddenly a criminal? I was just despondent, okay? I was melancholy. It happens. And after I reconcile a few things, this will all be done."

"What's 'a few things'?"

"Don't worry about it. I promise I won't leap off any structures," Jaxton replied bluntly before hanging up on his friend again.

"You asshole!" Cason yelled into his device.

Jaxton hastened out of the bathroom and jogged down the stationary escalators. He stopped in front of the Cole Haan store and saw a mannequin wearing an updated version of the blue Lunargrand wingtip shoes that he was wearing when he walked into Waverly's life.

"Hey? Did you get your technical equipment?" the guard in the red blazer asked.

"Got it. It's in the sling pack," Jaxton replied, zipping through the north-side revolving door and around the corner to 80 Columbus Circle.

He snuck right into the Mandarin Oriental, past a texting bellhop, and made his way into the futuristic elevators. Up he went until he arrived at the floor housing a modern restaurant of sophisticated American fare. Gone were the artistic touches, gracious service, and inventive cuisine. The stylish décor remained along with the stunning view of Columbus Circle and Central Park South. Jaxton approached the still romantically illuminated bar, opened the refrigerator, and grabbed a bottle of Dom Pérignon by the neck. He ripped out the cork to a rewarding pop and swigged the golden-hued, honeyed prestige cuvée. Seven years of aging undone in a guzzle, and Jaxton took up a seat next to the wall-sized window. He began to write as he drank.

> Exiting the handsome Columbus Circle Subway Station, I stepped into what was once the City of the Future, but now a city receding and swirling into economic gloom. The subways once consolidated the boroughs, but now bring the transient and undomiciled together like one apocalyptic party for the penniless. The captured nature of Central Park was rolled out before me like one aesthetic installation art project, replete with footbridges and arches, rustic woods, and romantic gazebos. The fairy-tale charm is now gone as no one is here to bask in its infallible design. Skyscrapers are kneeling, their heights a useless attribute as they are utterly uninhabited, their weekly pageant unceremoniously canceled. The city, once rising from the ocean, has regressed into the bedrock. What good are goliath-like structures if no one is around to ogle them? Will these tempestuous times galvanize New Yorkers to return more resilient and inventive and place them at the vanguard or will their place in history be eclipsed and the entire experiment relegated to the collapsed empire heap a la Rome and Egypt? The fires of capitalism have been doused, the mighty economic engine seized, and the entire concert of New York City silenced.

Jaxton waxed rhapsodic about New York as only he could. He continued to drain the Dom Pérignon bottle, feeling Fitzgerald-like as he tasted the stars. He was in the same hotel with virtually the same view as the night he took Adriana to Lincoln Center to experience *Swan Lake*. That night, he flipped a coin into the backlit Revson Fountain with a wish attached to it. That wish was never spoken, but it would be obtained nonetheless. Not with the inclusion of his romantic partner on that night but with the unforeseen spoiler, Waverly Larkin Bello.

Prior to that usurpation, the Mandarin Oriental was Jaxton's and Adriana's rendezvous point for their extravagant nights out. Adriana was, to him, something ethereal. She dominated the real estate market in Riverdale with a flawless combination of beauty, intellect, ambition, and likeability. She was content to love herself over having the wrong person love her. But Jaxton was adored by readers, in love with himself, and incapable of filling voids left behind by those less equipped. However, her vulnerable beauty still held dominion over him, and he was poised to grow into a role that would prepare him for marriage. He took a step back from Adriana after he learned he would have to shoulder more than just the standard burdens if he were to be with her.

Jaxton reminisced on one poignant conversation that they shared that was imbued with introspective insights on everything that stood in her way, namely herself.

"I'm adopted by white parents who raised me white. But I'm half Jamaican, half Italian," Adriana disclosed. "My fair skin always misleads people, and I get to hear their honest feelings about black people."

"What are their honest feelings about black people?" he asked naively.

"That they're inferior or they're ghetto or less than," she went on.

"Let me guess, they can't get state-issued ID cards to vote either? C'mon. What was this, twenty years ago?"

"No, 'til this day," she affirmed passionately.

"I'm not buying it," he countered. "At the risk of being that 'I love my black friends' guy, I love my black friends. I don't pigeonhole them. I don't apologize to them for society because they're doing well for themselves, and I don't view them as short-changed, oppressed, or inferior because they're not. And they don't view themselves that way either."

"Whether you want to admit it or not, we all have inherent biases," she continued. "I've heard people talk about the texture of my hair or the tone of my skin,"

"Who gives a shit. People have differences, and sometimes we highlight them. That's not racist. That's just observant. Your hair is straight and beautiful. Your skin is absolutely radiant. It has a caramel shade that makes it even prettier," he praised.

"Yeah, but those traits are preferred in society because they're seen as more European," she argued.

"My god. Who cares? Some will like curly, kinky, coarse hair and dark-colored skin, and some will like a woman who looks like a snowflake, and what does it really matter? Beauty is in the eye of the beholder. Self-pity and having a victim complex are things I detest."

"That easy for you to say. You're coming at it from a position of privilege," she declared.

"Privilege? Are you fucking kidding me?"

"Why are you cursing?" she asked through a yell.

"Because you are pissing me off! I have no privilege. I am Hispanic. My last name is Bello, and I'm brown."

"Which is not the same as black."

"Okay, a pork chop is not the same thing as a slice of bacon, but we can probably agree they're part of a similar thing," he stated.

"So Hispanics and Blacks are similar?"

"They're both not white. They're both minorities. They've both faced discrimination," he articulated, growing angrier with the conversation.

"But I'm part black. And I can tell you that discrimination against black people is worse."

"Sweetheart, you look white. Maybe someone might think you're Columbian or Puerto Rican but . . . the only thing black about you are your pumps."

"Oh, shut up, Jaxton!" she said, raising her voice even higher. "You're so insensitive and not at all empathetic. This is exactly what I'm talking about."

"I didn't even want to talk. I wanted to be intimate. You really thought that after we got undressed, it would be a good time to talk about certain baggage you're carrying? And by the way, it's difficult to delve into substantive issues when you have a full-blown erection,"

"You call that an erection?" she chastised.

"Not anymore. Your complex about being adopted and biracial and not having nappy hair gave me an early onset of erectile dysfunction."

"Fuck you!" she roared. "You better not even dream about getting any from me."

"Good because I can't afford a psychiatrist for you."

"You're an asshole. Do you know that? You probably do because you're *you*, and you seem to know fucking everything except you don't seem to really believe that black lives really matter!"

"Of course, black lives matter, but I don't have to put it on a goddamn T-shirt to prove it. Or do I need to buy a BLM shirt to satisfy your fickle opinion of me? I'm getting dressed. I think maybe this date is over," Jaxton deduced.

He collected his belongings and hastily moved to the bathroom. Adriana slumped in the bed, naked in so many ways. Fights like these slowly unraveled them and created the chasm that would be filled by his eventual wife and mother to his child.

Jaxton revived that tucked away moment and it seemed to sting him still. He achingly meditated on the past, momentarily forgetting that he was currently somewhat of a fugitive of the law. He gazed out at New York sensually, knowing that he wanted to take her in, but he was fleeing from her in the same breath like with Adriana. He was inebriated by drink, the Dom Pérignon affecting his senses and memory but motivated by his renewed energy for living. This was all galvanizing Jaxton and disconnecting him emotionally from the self-destructive actions of earlier that morning. He fielded a call from Cason.

"Hey, what level mobilization are you up to now?" Jaxton joked.

"Hey," Cason mimicked. "I'm done chasing you around the city. The helicopter returned to Brooklyn. I have to report to the Barclays Center for a protest."

"A protest? What the heck are they mad about now?" Jaxton posed.

"A cop in Minnesota killed an unarmed black man. He stepped on his neck for about nine minutes," he informed. "They have it all on cellphone video. It looks terrible. There's no justification for it, so . . . rightfully, people are pissed off."

"Okay, but that's Minnesota. The NYPD hasn't had any issues since the Staten Island incident," he stated. "What does that have to do with us here?"

"Come on, man, You know why. New York is a stage. This is where you come to be heard the loudest. Some financiers are supposedly backing them too. They're coming in on buses into Port Authority Bus Terminal. I'm responding to the mobilization point with forty-eight cops, and I'm only one of six sergeants. They got two lieutenants, a captain, and the duty chief," he revealed. "That's a level 2 mobilization, by the way, smartass. Don't think I didn't catch that."

"What about social distancing? They're going to protest six feet apart?"

"Social distancing is done. We're lucky if we can keep them six feet back from *us*," Cason replied.

"I have a feeling this is going to get dangerous. You know what? I'll meet you over there," Jaxton said, his urgency rising as he transitioned away from his role as the hunted.

"No. I told you, go home to Gracie and Waverly. They need to see you."

"I'm not ready to see them. Plus, they are not expecting me until the evening. How many people are they anticipating at this protest?"

"I don't know. They said between ten and thirty thousand," Cason replied.

"Thirty thousand! That's not a protest. That's a goddamn army. You said Barclays Center, right?"

"Go home, Jax! I can't worry about you and this detail at the same time."

Jaxton paused at that moment and pondered which way he should go. He had one foot in the past and one in the future. He stared out at the Columbus statue, which would soon become the subject of so much disdain and controversy. He took one last sip of champagne. The mechanics of dealing with a pandemic and quarantine seemed simple in comparison to what was about to transpire. For both men, life, as they knew it on recent terms, would once again change. The phone call concluded and few knew that they were on the cusp of a reckoning, a seismic societal shift, and a tidal wave of reform brought about by the perfect storm of isolation, destitution, injustice, and dearth in leadership. The moment was coming directly for them. This was their ring walk.

CHAPTER 5

Now Entering the Ring

It hit him suddenly though not unexpectedly. Like weaving through a boxing match and anticipating getting hit but not quite at the precise moment that he eats a hook. But he needed to get shellacked in order to be awakened from his somnambular state and reacquaint himself with an adage that he once lived by, "Protect yourself at all times." Jaxton had failed to protect his mental health and equanimity while penning weekly magnum opuses in the epicenter of crime, culture, commerce, and change. New York was at the vanguard and, certainly, once great but faltering mightily like a shot fighter taking a match he knew he had no chance of winning. Ironically, he was now reminded of his preeminence. It was his flaw in defense that put him tempestuously on the offensive. And it was in that truculent posture that he was at his best, stylistically knocking friends and foes alike on their asses unceremoniously and not giving a shit. Jaxton was about to undergo yet another metamorphosis. This was transitory, a pursuit of human dreams amid brewing chaos, unfettered by the structures of employment schedules or familial obligations. Jaxton held his breath against the magnitude of this moment. He set his sights on the shifting showdown at the Barclays Center. It was the home of a symbolic collision between the peacekeepers and the agitated and emboldened social justice mob. Jaxton dialed his wife.

"Waverly?" he greeted in a barely audible tone.

"Hi," his wife returned stoically. "How's work going?"

"Um . . ." Jaxon held back tears now. "It's going okay. I um . . ."—he took a long pause—"I have an assignment in Brooklyn, at Barclays Center."

"I thought all sports were canceled?"

"It's not sports. It's politics. The stakes are much higher," he elaborated. "It's a protest against police brutality."

"Did something happen in New York?"

"Not New York. Minneapolis. The cops there killed an unarmed black man. It was heartless, I was told. But you know, this is the biggest stage and all that. This is where their voices can be heard the loudest," he went on. "How's the princess doing?"

"She's good, missing her daddy. Waiting for you to come home and play My Little Pony with her."

"That's my favorite thing to do with her. Give her a big hug and a bunch of kisses from me. Tell her that Daddy loves and adores her and that she means more to me than sweet life itself. I'll be home tonight."

"Are you ready to start anew once you get home?" Waverly asked, admiring a photo magnet of the three of them on the refrigerator.

"I would love to make up and move forward if we can."

"Of course, we can. I love you and you love me . . . You love me, right Jaxton?"

"Mm-huh," Jaxton replied, producing a low affirmatory sound.

"Don't be ambivalent," she urged. "When things stop making sense, we'll figure it out."

The curtain was about to rise on one of the most spectacular and simultaneously heartbreaking acts in New York City history. Transcendent emotion filled the air on a day that would reverberate in the turbulent timeline of the city. One hundred and seventy-five years of policing in New York was about to come to a combustible climax.

A mass of people awaited the NYPD at what had suddenly become the impromptu Black Lives Matter headquarters, the Barclays Center. As police and protesters converged, divided by plain metal barricades, Jaxton sought to reconvene with Cason. If there was to be a reunion, it would be staged in the shadow of the political tsunami that was on the cusp of sweeping the nation and crumbling the cosmopolis.

Jaxton acclimated to being no longer the pursued, to once again having New York City as his untrammeled playground despite it still being closed, according to the ruling class. He did not yet know that sinister domestic forces were converging on New York City, intermixed with the Black Lives Matter contingent, donning inconspicuous urban camouflage. That the once intoxicating dreams of capitalism were being torn down by the anti-American culture of cancelation that saw any mistake as a reason to eliminate anyone or anything from its story. The city that once hurled itself unrestrainedly into the sky was about to disintegrate back into its base. The stage was being set for an act that no one foresaw during the city's pause during the pandemic as it was about to be opened by brute force and the sheer will of the people. The great land of opportunity was soon being prosecuted for its imbalances and inequities. Jaxton was determined to make it to Brooklyn and the Barclays Center to see how New York City would emerge from quarantine.

"I wonder," he pensively said to himself. "I wonder what New York City will do now."

Just wait and see what New York City will do during its great, unsilenced roar.

On his train ride to the Barclays Center, Jaxton watched a video of Waverly and him singing Happy Birthday to Grace and her blowing out a candle shaped like the number 2. That was the beautiful thing about technology: you could carry your most treasured memories in your pocket. He reflected on the joy in their home and how Grace's wit and timing could make laughter appear out of thin air. He recalled indelible conversations with her, which truly shaped his perspective as a father. It was a title he would wear like the Statue of Liberty wears her crown of seven spikes. And he would cross the seven seas if he needed to or move heaven and earth altogether to reunite with his child. He would even walk through hell as was the case here. He just had not seen the flames yet. Yes, all was quiet on his train ride except there was the voice of his young angel replaying in his head like an ethereal movie scene directed by unconditional love.

"Is it hard being small?" he recalled once asking Grace as she pouted, arms crossed.

"It's hard being small because everyone is bigger than you," she replied in her nasal voice. "And you have to ask for everything 'cause . . . 'cause you can't reach it b-be-cause it's so high up."

She tilted her head and scrunched up her nose like a bunny after saying this. Her childish tick of playing with her fingers while she spoke was an idiosyncrasy he found so endearing.

"You're so cute. You can't reach it just yet. But you're going to grow up and be able to reach things you never dreamed of," he assured, trying not to rush the most precious and shortest time in her life.

"I don't wanna grow up," she stated with conviction, stomping her foot.

"Well, I don't want you to grow up either. I want you to keep being my little baby. You have plenty of time to grow up and become great."

"Daddy," she said, followed by a long pause, "I'm not already great?"

The question hit him like a liver punch. He reflected for a good moment, feeling a responsibility to answer honestly and with something more than the usual generic parental lines aimed at appeasement and quieting children. Jaxton thought about his childhood, reminiscing on small, tender moments of meaning when an adult took the time to explain something more concretely to him. He had almost forgotten what kids go through, what it was like to be that size. He prepared his next statement like a president preparing his State of the Union address and dropped himself to her eye level.

"You know . . . greatness comes in all sizes. When you were born, you changed the dynamics . . . uh, the structure, the way our house was set up. Our whole lives really. You gave us an education in life, just your presence in ours. You were fussy, you didn't like eating, you didn't like sleeping. It seemed like you didn't really like it in our home. You challenged Mommy and me, tested our love, brought us to tears . . . brought us to our knees basically."

"I brought you to your knees?" she asked in her wondrous way. "Like when we're at church, Dad-dy?"

"Exactly like church, down to our knees. I always knew that kids were tenacious, uh *persistent*. But tending to your needs was basically a nonstop job that pushed your mother and me to the limit. And it took its toll. But then, I started to feel your love for me and that kept me pushing forward. Your dependent looks that said 'Daddy' before you could. You crying in my arms and finally going limp in my arms, all cried out. Little did you know that Daddy was crying too."

"You cried, Dad-dy?" she questioned with wide eyes.

"Daddy may have cried a tear or two," he replied sheepishly. "But then we went on daddy-daughter dates and took silly selfies, and I wore a tiara because . . . well, because you wanted me to."

"Daddy looked pretty in my tiara," she replied, accompanied by high-pitched giggles.

"Hardly. Scary is probably a better description. But as soon as you could walk, you were off to the races. You jumped into my arms off the couch, made me run after you at the pier, and made me chase away the monsters under the bed for you."

"I remember that, Dad-dy. You made those monsters disappear."

"They never stood a chance. You know, you belong to the world, but you belong to me. I was put on this planet to catch your falls and teach you how to be the best Grace that you can be. Your tiny breaths at night, the way you twirl in your tutu, and when you say, 'Giddy up, horsey'—these are the moments I live for," he revealed.

"You're a good horsey," she complimented giddily.

"Well, I may be a good horsey, but you're a great daughter. You are brave, you are funny, you are smart, you are . . .," Jaxton paused, becoming emotional, "you are perfect, baby."

"And you are a perfect, Dad-dy," she said, bringing him to tears.

"Well . . . perfect is better than great," he said, sniffling. "So yeah, you're great, sweetie. To answer your question, you are great already."

Jaxton had been warned by an older coworker that having children would bring him to his knees. He did not grasp the full breadth and scope of the advice until he himself was a parent. And this was truthful in multifold. He knelt to the level of his daughter to address her eye to eye, and it made her feel as if she were being heard. When she was younger, in moments of frustration when he could not get her to stop crying, he would feel helpless and at the mercy of his infant. She had brought him to his knees. And at night, while she dreamt and he proofread his articles for the magazine, he would genuflect and pray for her safety and security. He would do anything to ensure the health and happiness of his beloved daughter and kneeling before God was just part of the recipe, a big part. But his friend was right. Children bring you to that point. To be clear, those were the only times the pugilistic penman ever took a knee.

Jaxton blotted his tears as the subway car rumbled its way to Atlantic Avenue. He had his friend prominently on his mind and his daughter pulsating through his heart. Anticipation was growing. There was something heavy hanging over the air, and his friend, an NYPD sergeant at the eye of the tumult, was going to be front and center as everything unfolded. He emerged from the subway and bled into the masses. He could see the behemoth arena and its imaginative design, swooping panels of weathered steel cantilevering into a futuristic canopy. The digital façade flashed, "Barclays," prominently, but what struck Jaxton was the assortment of anti-police signs being held up by the thousands, seemingly all emerging from quarantine simultaneously to direct their anger at the police. "Fuck 12," "ACAB: All Cops Are Bastards," "The only good cop is a DEAD cop," and the old standby, "Fuck the Police," were all on display. Jaxton picked a sign off the ground. The anger was different than in previous demonstrations; it was more vile, sulfuric, tinged with a deep-rooted hatred for cops that seemed authentic. It was like everybody present believed that all of society's problems could somehow be attributed to the police. Jaxton sought help finding his friend but instantly realized that he was on unfriendly terrain. He instead attempted to use his press credentials to advance forward into the crowd and locate his companion himself.

"Excuse me, guys. Pardon me!" he repeated as he knifed through the crowd and moved closer to the sports venue. Chants of "Black lives matter" picked up and grew louder, rising in intensity. Jaxton was able to elbow his way to where a perimeter of metal barriers segregated the angry crowd from the police officers working the event.

"Officer, good afternoon," he began. "Can you help me?"

"Your sign says, 'FUCK 12' and you want my help? I'm sure one of these social justice warriors can assist you," the officer retorted.

"No, I'm not actually protesting," Jaxton revealed, discarding the sign. "My friend, Cason, uh excuse me . . . Sergeant Sax. He was trying to help me get home after I tried killing—"

"What?" the officer interjected. "Are you bugging?"

"Hear me out, Officer. I was feeling despondent. One of your supervisors, who is actually here somewhere, saved my life. I guess feeling suicidal is the proper way to phrase it although I've never admitted that to anyone until right now. Anyway, I'm rambling, but . . . Sergeant Sax is a friend of mine, and I'm worried about him in this climate of police hatred."

"Sergeant Sax. Yeah. He's the squad 3 supervisor," the officer began. "I *wish* he were my boss; the guy is a gentleman. He's here somewhere, but I doubt he's in any danger. That guy knows how to handle himself."

"What the fuck?" erupted the cop's partner. "Yo. Get back!"

In that instant, the crowd began pushing the metal barriers against the officers.

"Hey! What the hell are you doing! You're crushing me!" Jaxton yelled as he climbed over the barriers onto the law enforcement side.

"Get the fuck back on that side!" the officer yelled, shoving Jaxton.

"With all due respect, Officer, I can't! I need to see my friend, Cason."

Jaxton zigzagged into the platoon of officers and took at least a few elbows and a baton strike to the kneecap, adding a limp to his gait.

"I am not a damn protester!" Jaxton shouted as he twisted through. He bounced off numerous officers before stumbling right into the arms of a sergeant.

"You're under arrest, you goddamn psychopath," Cason declared, hugging his longtime mate. "You son of a bitch!"

"My mom was a saint. And I think it's time for us to both go home," Jaxton determined.

"'Go home?' Look at the size of this crowd, brother. This is my overtime you're looking at. This is my mortgage payment. I ain't going nowhere anytime soon," Cason informed.

"Well, then neither am I," Jaxton countered.

Rocks and bottles were now being hurled at the police officers and paintball rounds began to *pop* on some officers' uniforms. The cops, far outnumbered and underprepared, began to tactically retreat.

"SRG Sergeant, Central, I need more units to the Barclays Center! We need a 10-13! We're getting heavy airmail," Cason barked into his Motorola.

"What do we do?" Jaxton asked, his face now ghostly white.

"Stick with me, Jaxton!"

At that moment, the officers were forcibly pushed back toward the Barclays Center oculus, which somehow itself looking meek against the larger cityscape and salivating crowd. A police van was set ablaze by strategically placed fireworks and officers were rammed back by a stampeding horde, slamming down the metal barricades. Jaxton and Cason were separated after a bottle struck Jaxton in the head, and he dove for cover. It crossed Jaxton's mind that he might die on this day after all. Cason was wielding his baton to keep back the aggressors and ordered his officers to make numerous arrests. It was a tall order as arrestees violently resisted, knocking cops to the ground and easily escaping.

As dusk crept in, darkness would provide the perfect cover for acts of anarchy. A Molotov cocktail swirled through the air, its flames illuminated against hunchbacked streetlamps, and exploded onto a police vehicle. Chaos reigned at the foot of the Barclays Center, and Jaxton and Cason were permanently split up. More fireworks went off, and bricks were hurled through the air, impacting against police officers' riot gear helmets.

There would be some controversy as to who placed those pallets of bricks there. Conspiracy theories claimed it was the government so that the protests could descend into chaos and undermine the movement. Others claimed an old Hungarian billionaire had funded the insurgency in hopes of disrupting American society. It was likely well-prepared anarchists taking advantage of strained police resources and implementing a system where bricks could be transported via rented vans to provide ammunition for insurgents. The whole picture had degenerated into something diametrically opposed to a peaceful protest.

It has been said that supporting Black Lives Matter and law enforcement are not mutually exclusive. But on this night, it was impossible for both these entities to coexist. Violence had become the chosen vocabulary of that nocturne, and the lexicon was understood loud and clear and without even modest equivocation.

Night properly fell, and police transmissions for help could be heard on the radio the entire night. Garbage cans were lit on fire, additional police vehicles were ignited, and rioters pelted the police with anything they could get their hands on. Police batons were again waved menacingly in retaliation to the onslaught. Polycarbonate cracked against bone as blood painted the sidewalk in Pollock-like splatters. Glass shattered from bottles, from police car windows, from local businesses being vandalized. It was as if the broken windows theory, campaigned against by Mayor Wilhelm, but right then eviscerated in earnest, was being proven in real time. Graffiti and criminal mischief gave way to robbery and arson. It was surreal to see the Cable News Network cover this event as a peaceful protest, considering Jaxton, an actual journalist of the award-winning ilk, was on the scene as things turbulently transitioned into wreckage.

Jaxton rose from under a vehicle, trickling blood and realizing that he was opening his eyes to a new reality, like the characters in *Endgame* after an apocalyptic disaster. The tone, theme, and paradigm had completely shifted in that bloody, firelit clash at Barclays Center. The scene had devolved into a riot and, suddenly, "Defund the police" had become a chorus and a social media hashtag, picking up all types of momentum. The hero first responders from the coronavirus pandemic had instantly become the scapegoats for all of society's ills again. A heartless officer, in a small Midwestern city, had set off a tsunami of anti-police sentiment, perhaps dormant after previous high-profile police-involved deaths, but perpetually brewing.

Jaxton picked up the base shard of the bottle that had, presumably, knocked him to the ground and put it in his messenger bag with his other collected keepsakes. He was, once again, an embedded journalist and felt a sense of purpose to cover this story authentically. He was no longer doting on the beautiful, romantic New York of the previous one hundred years. He was now penning a work about the new New York, partly of Mayor Wilhelm's disastrous policies, and what would balloon to a mind-boggling 700 percent increase in shootings in the Big Apple. Newly enacted Bail Reform legislation put many of these perpetrators right back on the street to victimize again.

In the weeks to come, parents would be killed in front of their children, and children would be killed in front of their parents. The movement would be silent on the murder of a one-year-old Brooklyn boy, shot while sleeping in his stroller, instead choosing to focus on the police. One of their mottos was, "The only good cop is a dead cop." This slogan stood in stark contrast to what Jaxton knew most police officers to be. He hearkened back to the day his friend saved a perfect stranger's life and did so with patience, empathy, and compassion that seemed like superpowers when wielded by the NYPD sergeant. As Jaxton gathered himself and figured out a way to locate Cason in the awakened city, his mind traveled back to the moment his friend became a lifesaver atop a scorching rooftop a half-decade prior to this opening salvo.

CHAPTER 6

The Life That Matters

A 911 call had been placed describing a male pacing back and forth on the ledge of a South Bronx housing project rooftop. Cason, with Jaxton performing a ride-along in a radio motor patrol vehicle, was anticipating a lazy morning as things usually did not pick up until around noon.

"It's probably just an NYCHA employee having a smoke," Cason downplayed as he sharply reclined as he drove the police car to the location at ice cream truck speed.

"Yeah, but why would he be on the ledge? There's plenty of room on the roof to enjoy a loosie," Jaxton reasoned.

"I don't know. Maybe he wanted to get a better view of the city."

"That beautiful, majestic city, right?"

"Units, does anyone have eyes on the jumper?" the central dispatcher asked urgently.

"Five-one sergeant, Central, is this a *confirmed* jumper?"

"Um, let me read the job again . . . It's unconfirmed, Sergeant, but I am receiving multiple calls now," the dispatcher disclosed. "Any units made contact with the male as of yet?"

"Central, I'm 84 at the location. I'll check and advise," Cason replied.

Jaxton and Cason hustled into the elevator; the cab was already parked in the lobby, and they stepped over a puddle of minutes-old urine. Jaxton repeatedly smashed the button to the thirty-first floor. The ride up was slow and unsteady, and the doors ultimately opened with the doorframe and the landing badly misaligned. The duo hopped up and dashed toward the A staircase, springing up the steps with urgency before plowing the door open against a deafening alarm wail. They scanned 360 degrees of the black tar project rooftop, canopied under resplendent blue skies. In the southwest corner of the roof, on the street side of the ledge, a slim black man, shirtless and hopeless, straddled the railing with a precarious posture and utter resignation. Cason stepped into the moment and immediately engaged the man.

"Good morning, young man. I'm Sgt. Cason Sax. How are you feeling today?" Jaxton immediately took out a notepad to commence his role as an impromptu stenographer.

"Yo. How does it look like I'm feeling, bro?" the male replied. His arms were pulled behind him as they held the railing, knuckles up, and the 90-degree angle of the roof corner cut his V-shaped back directly in half.

"I don't know. It's a beautiful day, and you strike me as a strong, healthy guy with a lot of great attributes, so I'm just wondering what it is you're doing on the ledge."

"What do you think I'm doing? I don't want to live anymore, man. Nobody asked for no five-oh here, so let me just do what I gotta do," the male insisted, taking a long look at the street below as if visualizing the collision of body and pavement.

"What's your name, brother?" Cason asked compassionately, his arm extended as if reaching for him.

"Come on, man. Fuck outta here. I ain't telling you shit," the distressed man replied.

"Hey, I need to know your name, so I can tell the world your story once everything is resolved. So who do I say the young man with a world of talent at his fingertips was?"

This elicited a slight smile from the male.

"I saw that," Cason informed. "I saw you smile, my man."

"You funny, my nigga. I didn't smile, but I see what you were trying to do. I give you props."

"I don't need props. I need your name. I'm sure you have a super cool name, man. What's your name, brother? I bet your name is like . . ."

"Life," the man disclosed, pride overpowering his stubbornness.

"Life?"

"Everyone calls me Life," the male reiterated, stretching his arms out as he yawned ahead of an outburst of unintelligible sound.

"Tired, huh? Is Life a moniker or your given birth name?"

"Okay, now you're asking too many questions, man."

"Okay, okay. My bad," Cason replied with a nervous laugh. He turned to glimpse Jaxton's facial expressions and read how he was handling the ordeal.

At that moment, Jaxton passed Cason his notepad with the words, "Do we need to call anyone?" scrawled on it. Cason looked at the pad, then back at Life and wrote, "HNT, ESU, TARU."

"Yo. What are you writing over there?"

"Grocery list. If we stay up here for a while, I have to make sure my assistant, my little gopher over here, brings my lady the milk and eggs that she ordered me to pick up. You know how females get."

"Tell me about it," Life agreed with a smirk. "But you ain't gon be up here long. I'm ending this real shit quick, my dude, before all the news vans get here."

"Central, let me get hostage negotiations, emergency services, and TARU over here forthwith. We have a confirmed man on a ledge," Jaxton transmitted discreetly as Cason worked on his subject.

"My man, how can a guy named Life be contemplating death? That's too much of a paradox. You're young, good-looking, I bet you could even spit bars for days—"

"How did you know I was a rapper?"

"With a moniker like that, I could tell you're philosophical and profound. You are either a poet or a rapper. Either way, it's lyricism, which is all about telling a story, which brings me back to telling *your* story, my brother."

The man on the ledge took a moment to collect his thoughts while again looking down at the vehicles traveling briskly on the busy Bronx avenue below.

"The story of Life is about a man who took the plunge. The end. Wait. Who came from nothing, had nothing, and left with nothing," the man dictated with fierce finality.

"That's not true. The story of Life is about a man who had the world at his fingertips. Who got up off the canvas, who literally came back from the ledge, and resurrected his . . . life. He didn't resurrect after death like Jesus did. He resurrected while he was alive, which speaks volumes about his resolve and his fortitude."

"Yo, I swear. This nigga is good! Bro, you should be on television saying shit like that. You would really have some other nigga believing that shit."

"It's because I believe in you. I mean it. A man named Life meeting his demise like this is not just paradoxical, it's . . . it is oxymoronic."

"You a thesaurus, dude? Got big-ass words."

"And you've got big-ass dreams, which you can only achieve if you come down from that ledge," Cason argued. "Come down off that ledge, and maybe Life and DJ Case Money can do a collabo."

"Stop it, bro! Collabo? A guy like you doesn't collaborate with a guy like me. I'm a perp to you if you saw me on the street. A black male with saggy pants, so I'm nothing but a suspect. I know you're working. You're getting paid for this. I don't matter to you. You're just doing a job. It's a *job*. Now you do it well, I'll give you that. But you're getting bread for this shit. You're not doing it outta the goodness of your heart or because you really care about me. I'm just some nigga in the ghetto looking for attention to you."

"Man, I'll clock out right now and prove to you that I care about you. You matter to me. Your life matters to me," he proclaimed as a connection with Life was organically forming under the sizzling sun.

Life twisted a braid that had come loose behind his right ear.

Cason prosecuted his case as the rooftop gradually filled with NYPD personnel. The emergency service unit, the hostage negotiation team, and a surveillance and intelligence unit known as TARU, chiefs with two and three stars on their uniform all occupied the summit right then. Cason looked over his shoulder at the sea of blue that was now there for Life, to talk him off that ledge and demonstrate to him that his life really did matter.

"Well, now it's a fucking party, ain't it?" Life noted. "When the dudes with the white shirts and the sticks up their asses get here, shit just got real."

"It ain't a party until you come off that ledge, and we could really start the celebration," Cason replied.

Everybody on that rooftop was baked under 98-degree heat. Emergency services, outfitted with all their heavy equipment, helmets, shields, and rappelling cables, sweated out their body heat in pools of moisture. Portions of their uniforms darkened with precipitation. Jaxton remained there, cooking under that heat, boiling, dripping sweat onto his curling notepad.

He ripped out wet pages that bled out the ink of the keywords and phrases that he was writing down to memorialize this.

"Do you want to take over?" Cason asked, turning to the commanding officer of the hostage negotiation team, a lieutenant in a windbreaker raid jacket.

"No, you've got a good rapport. You are wearing him down. Just offer him something,"

"Hey, what's that old nigga sayin'? He telling you to shoot me?" Life interrogated, separating his body from the brick ledge as if doing a backward pushup.

"Don't do it!"

"I was just stretching. Chill, Case. You've been calm until now. Don't fuck it up."

"No way. No way, brother. We ain't fucking this up. The lieutenant was just asking me if I thought you were thirsty. It's sweltering up here, man. You need a beverage?"

"Ya got vodka?" Life asked, letting out a villainous cackle behind it.

"Can't drink on the job. We got hard water on the rocks though."

"You a funny cat. Shit, but now that you mention it . . . a nigga' is sweating bullets, no pun intended ha!"

"No pun, no pun," Cason replied. "These guys brought some water for you. I got you."

"I'm telling you right now, if any one of those big niggas in SWAT gear gets close to me, I am jumping off this fucking roof."

"Nobody is getting close to you except for me—"

"Nah, I don't want you close to me either. Throw the water," he ordered.

"If I throw the water, I mean, shit, I haven't played baseball in years. I might throw it wide, and you'll have to reach for it. I don't want you slipping off the roof because of my shitty arm. I'll walk it over to you."

"No, Sarge, you aren't strapped in. You can't go over to him. It's too big of a safety risk," a senior member of emergency services instructed.

"So how do we get the water to him?" Cason whispered.

"You fuckers better stop whispering over there! I'm about to leave this earth!"

"Hey, what's up brother? I'm Officer Tapia from Emergency Services. You and the sarge have been engaged in this beautiful dialogue, and I'm not trying to interfere in any way, but we can't risk the good sergeant over here slipping and going over that ledge. So I'm going to put the water in the claw here, and you just grab it when it gets to you, okay?"

"The claw, huh? Ya'll niggas have all the gadgets and gizmos, don't you? Ya'll be on some futuristic shit, right? I'm surprised ya boys ain't throw a fucking net on me that tightens like in Batman and shit or maybe fly a drone over to me."

"The drone is charging. Short battery life," Cason joked. "But nah, man. It's not that serious. We can just use this rod that extends. Old people use this shit to put on their tennis shoes."

"Yo. You wildin'. Sergeant Sax, you a funny dude. You know that?"

"Reyna doesn't think so," Cason replied, as Officer Tapia approached with the water bottle secured in the grip of the device.

Life removed the water bottle and uncapped it. Members of emergency services slowly inched forward, their rappelling cables anchored onto pipes on the ground, the ropes and clasps all engaged to ensure their safety.

Life tilted his head back and took a long swig of water. He closed his eyes, and he enjoyed the hydrating comfort of ice-cold water entering his digestive system. He squeezed the water bottle in one hand and the roof railing in the other. Participants on the apex could almost see his body temperature lowering with each swallow of the refreshing liquid. Each sip bought them a little more time.

"Ahhh," Life let out in relief.

His thirst was quenched, and his life was momentarily simple. But he was still melancholy, and he was about to be swarmed by a gang of six-foot-tall ESU officers ready to rip him back from danger into the realm of safety. They all pounced on Life, grabbed his shoulders, and snatched him from the ledge onto burning hot roof tar.

"You fuckin' snakes!" Life yelled as ESU members struggled to place the handcuffs on him. You betrayed me, Sergeant Sax!" he accused, refusing to bend his arms behind his back.

"I didn't betray you," Cason replied into his ear. "I genuinely care for you as a human. I got love for you, man."

"You fucking lied!"

"I didn't lie. I told you your life mattered. And this was my way of showing you."

Cason quickly kissed Life's forehead as ESU members smothered him and restrained him in handcuffs. Jaxton scribbled notes on his pad as quickly as humanly possible.

"Is this sort of an everyday thing?" Jaxton questioned.

"Oh yeah, just another day at the office . . . A down day, in fact. Feet up," Cason replied.

"Hey, Sergeant Sax," Life beckoned as he was slowly raised back onto his feet.

"What's up, my brother?"

"Did you really mean it?"

"What specifically? I mean . . . I meant all of it, but what are you referring to?" he asked.

"My life actually matters to you?" Life questioned.

"Your life is important. Yes, it matters to me. *You* matter, Life. That's why I wanted to save you. I hope we meet again under better circumstances."

"Me too. You're a good cop. Not all you guys are bad," Life credited.

No one knew it at the time, but the debate regarding whose life matters would go on to become *the* political phrase of its day. "Black lives matter" would somehow be diametrically opposed by "All lives matter," and "Blue lives matter" would become a rallying cry countering the anti-police sentiment but perceived as a racist phrase by members of the BLM movement. None of that mattered to Cason, who was virtually apolitical and genuinely valued people on a human level as demonstrated by the care, compassion, and patience that he extended to Life.

"God bless you, brother," Cason offered, as Life was led away in handcuffs. "You're not under arrest. We're just going to take you to the hospital to receive some psychiatric help. The handcuffs will come off once you get triaged."

Cason was soon alone on the roof with Jaxton. They looked out at postcard-worthy New York City and its sun-melted horizon line.

"It's lonely at the top," Jaxton remarked.

"Indeed." Cason smirked with satisfaction.

"You have to write up a report on this?" Jaxton asked.

"Yeah. I'll bang it out. No big deal."

"The view from up here is unreal."

"All that's missing now is a cigar."

"Damn, I should have picked some up," Jaxton replied. "You don't have any?"

"Not on me. I smoked my last one yesterday."

"I owe you one. Take this as an IOU from me. We'll find a good reason to smoke again."

"Do I need to save another life to get a stogie, Jax?"

"That's the criteria," Jaxton replied. "So we'll probably be lighting up by the weekend."

"While the city burns, we'll burn cigars," Cason forecasted.

"You have a real gift for this."

"I don't have a gift for anything."

"You're a hero, Case."

"No, brother. I'm just a cop. I barely made supervisor. I took an oath to serve and protect. Sometimes that entails protecting people from themselves."

Jaxton took note of everything that transpired on that rooftop that morning and would go on to write a column about the NYPD titled, "New York Pretty: Cops Hold the Beauty of the City Together with Heart and Soul." It would be read by hundreds of thousands of New Yorkers and increase Jaxton's profile as one of the preeminent writers of all things New York. Admiration for cops was not exactly at its post-911 zenith back then as the controversial "stop and frisk" policy had been declared racist by its detractors. However, appreciation for Jaxton's writing had, contrastingly, hit its critical pinnacle. But more so than just propelling Jaxton into a new echelon as a writer, the save on the rooftop propelled Cason into virtual immortality in Jaxton's eyes. He had literally watched Cason save a man's life, and the man's name *was* Life. It could not get any more poetic or allegorical than that.

With a deep-rooted belief in Cason's goodness, Jaxton set out to locate him in a city that was witnessing the cover of night used against it as a cloak for maelstrom and malfeasance. Jaxton overheard a dissident stating that he was getting ready to loot the stores in SoHo and saw a band of agitators walk toward the subway station. The group was furnished with crowbars, giant monkey wrenches, construction hats, and backpacks with an assortment of burglar's tools inside. He knew Cason would be in the eye of the storm, and so he sought it out, knowing he would find his courageous friend in the middle of the biggest moment in recent New York City history. What would New York do when it once again had its back pressed against the wall?

Jaxton was to board the iron horse for a distinct part of New York City. Once the preeminent laboratory of contemporary life and a city of the future, New York was about to be thrust back into the past to deal with demons that were never fully put to rest. Jaxton too had not completely reconciled with his history, plunging into a love affair with Waverly as soon as the magic that he and Adriana had captured in a bottle had dissipated over differences in the way they carved their identities and defined themselves.

And then there was the matter of the suicide attempt that now seemed like years ago. Jaxton had gone from swaying off the George Washington Bridge to witnessing people want to tear down George Washington within twelve hours. He would take in masterpieces at the MOMA, retrace his footsteps on *The Great White Way*, relieve his life in semicircular fashion at the grand Columbus Circle traffic vortex, and get knocked to the ground like a faded fighter at the footstep of the futuristically gargantuan Barclays Center. Jaxton got off the mat because he wanted to repay Cason for giving him the unrepayable gift of a second lease on life. He would commence on this venture defiantly, ignoring the blood on his brow and the stones and glass that now encircled him. He would see bright yellow circles designating the N, Q, and R trains, and so he ventured underground and traveled to what would be New York City's ground zero all over again.

Entr'acte

On his ride to SoHo, Jaxton traveled down the avenues of his most treasured memories, to the exact moment Waverly won over his heart. It originated at the very Barclays Center where the hostilities had just commenced. On that day, five years ago, the premier R and B singer of this generation, a songbird of rare emotional weight and pain, was belting cathartically, "I love you, I want to, share the rest of my life with you. If I can, but you can't, how can I go on? How can I go on, baby? I'm fallin' down. I'll still be lovin' you after I hit the ground."

Back then, the couple looked at one another with the future glistening in their eyes and their body heat mutually rising in affinity. They could visualize what was coming before it arrived, indicating true desire in their hearts. The concert took them through a labyrinth of emotions; past previously dormant chambers; and into the state of curiosity, magnetism, longing, and uncertainty. They would proceed afterward to Rockaway Beach and spend hours there getting to know one another and lay the foundation to something more substantial. In her car, she had a Brut sparkling wine from the Napa Valley and homemade chocolate-covered strawberries. Her intentions were transparent. She set up a picnic blanket with two small lanterns and unpacked her tasty delicacies. Ripe, juicy white grapes; plump, bright red strawberries coated in deep dark chocolate; the seductive bubbly; and her own sugary charm.

All would be consumed on that beach against the backdrop of undulating waves and a reflective orange moon. The sound of water rolling over packed yellowish-brown granulation both soothed and invigorated them. The five-and-a-half-mile boardwalk, which normally drew throngs, and the vast sandy expanse were entirely theirs. The sparkling wine diminished clarity and inebriated thinking. The night swirled like an impressionist mural. Emotions climbed and eyes swelled passionately as lower lips dropped desirously. Between conversation and consumption and carnality, their mouths met for an unforgettable kiss as waves broke on the shore. They transferred affection, exchanged the essences of sparkling wine on their palates, and melted into one another. Their aroused breaths and enchanted eyes carried them forward on a thin layer of cloud underneath their blanket. The magic carpet ride had commenced, and all past lovers had henceforth fallen by the wayside like vanquished soldiers and historical irrelevancies.

When they arrived at their hotel, they jumped into the pool with their clothes on and shared a breathtaking kiss underwater. It was a magical moment conjured up intrinsically and occurring under the cinematic light of the moon. Their futures intertwined as they entangled underwater, unable to be untwined even if they tried.

Jaxton reminisced and rode the metro, old and decrepit, to the site of what would become a chronicled showdown in SoHo. He rose from the underground and observed a polychromatic-graffiti-covered city that resembled nothing close to the city of tomorrow. Cities need to be allowed to flourish, to thrive, to thrust forward into the next decade. New York, contrarily, was now stagnant, putrid, and held hostage by an insatiable gang led by the incompetent mayor Wilhelm and his socialist-leaning sycophants. Jaxton arrived at Greene Street, his head swiveling and looking for his friend amid a sea of demonstrators, signs, and urban matter. New York was benighted, and the darkness would make it even more difficult for Jaxton to reunite with his endangered friend.

"Cason! Hey, Cason!" Jaxton yelled, drowned out by alternating chants of "Fuck the police" and "I can't breathe." He searched for his friend as storefront windows shattered and trash can bonfires sparked, their embers scattering into the night. Marxist symbols were spray-painted over everything that the vandals could coat in their aerosolized cans of rebellion. The radio transmissions that night presaged danger like never before. One by one, business facades were demolished by skateboards, bricks, and crowbars, brandished by "protesters." Outnumbered police officers raced to the scene to what was beginning to resemble a war zone. Some rebels amid the masses launched pyrotechnics at responding police. They looted Coach handbags, Rolex watches, Steve Madden shoes, and Apple phones. Jaxton was pinballing through this pandemonium, trying not to collide with those immersed in the disorder as he searched for Cason. Few wore masks. It seemed coronavirus's reign over the city had been usurped by something less out a science laboratory and more out of a social laboratory, perhaps even a classroom.

Despair now crept in as Jaxton's breaths were altered by emotion. New York was completely kinetic, but its movements were no longer beautiful. It was a brutish ballet and Jaxton yearned for the gentler, more graceful days of pleasant choreography. And then a woman, fearless and statuesque, caught his eye as the only static thing on the block. She stood on the corner of Prince Street, holding a simple black sign with white block lettering that read, "Black Lives Matter." Her chestnut mane blew dramatically in the wind, its medium reddish tones highlighted by the perimeter of fire that encircled her. A pair of gem-shaped light-almond-colored eyes entranced above the surgical mask protecting her precious mouth and straight Romanesque nose. Jaxton walked up to her and was immediately imprisoned by her gaze. He slowly inched toward her, invited almost, and she froze at her point on the street, which seemed all but staged. Both lowered their masks simultaneously as looks of recognition emerged in perfect synchrony. Incredulous smiles bloomed.

"Jaxton?" she asked, angling her face at his distinct features. "No fucking way!"

"*Adriana*? This can't be real. What are you doing here?" he questioned as she lowered her sign and moved toward what seemed the next, natural step, an embrace with her former lover.

Jaxton took a long stride in and threw both arms around her graceful, athletic shoulders. She snuck her arms underneath his and welcomed the sign of endearment. He squeezed her tightly, and she clung to him like a fatigued swimmer clinging to a pool wall.

"I've missed you. I think of you often," Jaxton confessed.

"You think of me often?"

The two took a moment to completely take the other in with the fresh eyes that the passage of time gifts its lovers.

"I do. And I don't know why things didn't work out with us. I've always believed you were otherworldly. Your beauty is so transcendent. I mean this is unreal—pinch me. Why did I meet you here now?" he asked, stream of consciousness in full effect.

"You're pinched. And that's a lot of . . . points to address at once. I think we were just too different. I've always thought you were special too. You are amazing in your own way. And I honestly don't know why or how God led us to this exact street today."

"To reconcile?" he guessed.

"Reconcile? You never called me. I told Cas—"

"I couldn't. I couldn't call you back then."

"I get it. And now here we are, Jax. We are *here*."

Jaxton and Adriana ignored glass breaking, sirens blaring, and police lines pushing back rioters around them. Their entire history was revisited in a glance and the look that was exchanged carried weight far beyond ordinary glances. As the city burned around them and the Black Lives Matter movement, supported by Antifa saboteurs, clashed with the Thin Blue Line, Jaxton and Adriana leaned into one another. Gravity pulled them, centimeters separated them, and their faces were brought into natural communion. They coalesced in unexpected lip-lock years delayed but, nevertheless, galvanizing. It was a transitory, enchanted moment, and it quickly vanished like their once mutual dreams. As they pulled apart, the dermis of their lips momentarily stuck together and their affection turned angry.

"Why didn't you ask me to marry you?" she questioned, grooming her hair with one hand, still auditioning, then pointing a finger fiercely into his face.

"I don't know. You had certain issues that I thought would always undermine us. I didn't realize then that you were supernatural. I didn't realize you were . . . extraterrestrial."

"You're calling me an alien? C'mon, Jax. Save the bullshit for your audience. I'm just a regular girl . . . But I am a good girl."

"No, you're not *just* a girl. You are spectacular. You are . . . something different. You are a constellation wrapped inside a galaxy."

"What?" she asked through a sweet girlish giggle. "You're always so over the top."

"I mean the universe. What's bigger? The universe or the . . ."

"I don't know. It's all interstellar, my love," she replied before correcting herself. "I didn't mean to call you my love. I meant to say . . . I probably said it in the generic sense—"

"It's okay, my love," Jaxton pardoned as he grabbed her face and pulled her in for one more tectonic kiss.

"I'm still your love?"

He confirmed it by returning to her alluring lips.

"You're married," she reminded.

"I can't deny that."

"Do you want to deny it?" she asked, separating from him.

The two exhaled deeply and realized that their history may forever remain abridged. He pulled her close to his heart in an embrace that would reverberate in their timeline.

"But you *do* love me?" she confirmed.

"*Yes*. Forever, even if we cannot ever be," he declared conclusively.

She processed his answer and pierced him with a look of longing.

"Why are you down here?"

"Because Cason is down here."

"Do you know where he is?"

"SoHo. That's all I know. He's here somewhere—Shit. This crowd is fucking rabid!"

"Well, let's find him," she replied, pounding her fist into her palm. "He's a cop. I see crimes being committed all around us. He can't be far."

Jaxton and Adriana held hands and ran through what felt like hellfire and brimstone. Porous stores gushed opportunistic pillagers. Merchandise spilled out through pulverized windows as mannequins lay strewn along debris-filled sidewalks. Night had fallen and swathed New York in violence not seen in decades. Coronavirus had effectively conceded to riots and Jaxton pursued Cason with equal ferocity. Adriana interlocked fingers with Jaxton and their story appeared to receive one last great dance amid the blazing metropolis.

"We will find him," she assured, squeezing his hand optimistically.

"He's got to be here. He always told me, 'Go to the belly of the beast. That's where it's safest.' In the belly of the beast everything is falling around you, but you're safe if you're right at the center of it all."

He squeezed her hand back.

"So that's where we'll go."

The two ran in sync, hoping to close the staggering day by venturing into the whirlpool of a city flung back into the past, not to the great prosperity of the late 1990s when the Dow Jones rocketed, but to the early '90s crime wave when murders soared to 2, 245. The dichotomy was blindingly stark. Jaxton would come eye to eye with something commensurate with his darkest fears that night. He went from begging to die earlier that morning to trying like hell to make sure he lived to tell his story. It would be an exhilarating, often harrowing, night set against the spiraling New York sky that appeared to move the way Van Gogh's most celebrated work appears kinetic to its spellbound admirers.

CHAPTER 7

City on Fire

Streetlamps backlit the carnage as blue-and-white police vehicles streaked down graffitied streets and fireworks cascaded and crackled, ricocheting off their bullet-resistant windows. The masses had come equipped with crowbars and hammers, ropes and helmets, gasoline and lighters, not items intrinsic to a peaceful demonstration. Rocks, bottles, and paintball rounds also pelted the patrol cars as they arrived on the scene. Some of the gaudiest, most opulent, and ostentatious stores were being ransacked on a scale not recallable. The storefronts of name-brand labels were now being reduced to rubble by the masses. New York was again an exporter, a mass producer of violence and fear.

It would later be told by the delusional Mayor Wilhelm that these were "mostly property crimes committed by a small cluster of nonpeaceful protesters." A sergeant on the scene—not Sergeant Sax—would counter that by quipping, "If property crimes were committed in Mogadishu, then sure, that's the case." The supervisor would be disciplined by the police commissioner for speaking to the media, the same media that used "fiery but mostly peaceful protests" as a headline on a chyron as a field reporter nervously broadcast from in front of a blazing building.

About a block away, in a darkened alley, Jaxton and Adriana encountered a cop, his head down and flanked by his trembling hands. The officer's legs were stretched out of the passenger seat of his RMP and dangling into the gutter.

"Excuse me, Officer?" Jaxton asked gingerly.

"What do you want? To tell me that black lives matter? Yeah, I know," he growled.

"Yeah, we all know that. And I think we can communicate that without burning down our city."

"Finally, somebody who gets it," the cop noted.

"Would you happen to know where Sgt. Cason Sax is, Officer? He's in SRG, whatever that means."

"Of course, strategic response group. You know Cason?"

"He's probably my best friend," Jaxton disclosed, showing the cop a picture of them on his phone.

"Yeah, that's him! He was in my company in the academy. Hell of a guy."

"Yeah, he's amazing," Adriana interjected. "Is he here somewhere?"

"Let me check," the officer replied, clicking his radio. "Central, it's one post six. Can anyone advise the location of SRG 2?"

After a few seconds, a transmission followed.

"SRG 2 sergeant, Central. Be advised, we're at Herald Square engaged with about two hundred protesters, not orderly at this time."

"Holy shit! That was Cason. That's his voice," Adriana confirmed.

"It is him. That's our friend."

"Do you guys know how to get to Herald Square?"

"I'm a New Yorker," Jaxton returned with pride.

Jaxton and Cason's friendship had unfurled like a pennant across the decade. It emerged from a city, which beheld their bond like a gem in its palm. New York, in its cultured preeminence, fielded these two working-class men like infielders at Yankee Stadium sprinting out to patrol the diamond. In their eyes, they were Jeter and A-Rod holding the Big Apple by its stem for imminent consumption and devouring of its ingratiated perks. The writer and the sergeant made one another, and New York, better.

At that moment, Jaxton and Adriana sprinted to the yellow-line subway station. They would catch the R train to Thirty-Fourth Street and, hopefully, have a reunion with their friend. On that train, they consumed each other visually as they travelled to the world's most famous department store.

"Did you ever think we would get this moment?" Adriana asked, her lush lips almost naturally puckered.

"No. I didn't actually think I'd ever see you again. Maybe it—this—was destiny."

"Destiny as in we were always meant to have this last, dramatic, miraculous moment?" she asked.

"Perhaps we were," he acquiesced, pulling her in for a hug, its enjoyment undermined by its inappropriateness.

Little did the two know that they were stepping into a referendum on American policy for the last twenty years. After the collective roar of an angry population would be vociferously let out, a defining question had to be posed, "What had been lost? And how much had been gained?" It was a question that would define the 2020 presidential election and set the stage for Americans to roar that unforgettable November of that transcendent year. But would that roar come from the vocal or the silent? A reconciliation between the two was effectively a mandate if the US were to sustain itself.

"Next stop, Thirty-Fourth Street, Herald Square," the conductor announced.

Jaxton and Adriana turned to each other with a sense of trepidation. Their reunion, long postponed, was transpiring under a set of circumstances not forecasted. The train doors opened, uncovering a portal to a dematerialized moment in time.

"Let's go!" Jaxton shouted, pulling Adriana by the arm as he had once pulled her out of a bar and into a relationship. As they glimpsed the world-famous Macy's brick face and the unilluminated Believe sign, they raced to the street used as a pavilion for the Thanksgiving Day parade marching bands and Santa Claus's grand finish. In the center of it all, almost cinematically, an NYPD van billowed smoke after lawbreakers had ignited it with a Molotov cocktail. Jaxton and Adriana moved swiftly through the perilous terrain, careful not to appear to be contributing to the anarchy so as not to end up on the business end of an officer's wrath. And there stood Cason with six other cops, surrounded by the rabid crowd.

"Get back!" he yelled, jabbing out his baton with both arms extended.

"That's him . . . Cason!" Adriana called out, pushing a few rioters aside. "Cason get the fuck outta there!" she implored.

"They're going to think you're one of these anarchists," Jaxton cautioned. "Sergeant Sax! Cason, get them off you!"

"Fuck the pigs! Fuck the pigs!" the crowd chanted, surging in volume as officers radioed for backup.

"SRG sergeant, Central, Give me a 10-13 to Macy's on Thirty-Fourth Street! We're severely outnumbered, and we're receiving heavy airmail. We got about two hundred protesters, not orderly at this time. Get us some additional units here, Central!"

Jaxton and Adriana were so close to their friend and had to helplessly watch him perform under fire. Projectiles pelted off his disorder control helmet's face shield as he and his officers held the line and warded off the insurrection.

"Central, more units forthwith!" Cason repeated as they had their backs pressed to the department store's famous windows, giving explicit verbal commands to angry agitators to cease their criminality.

"Cason, get the fuck out of there!" Jaxton begged, at that point physically moving people. "Hey, stop this shit!"

Cason turned his head to give instructions to his patrolmen, and a young man in a pro-socialism shirt broke through the police line. He raised a brick into the air and, in an instant, smashed it against Cason's riot gear helmet before running away.

"*Cason!*" Jaxton howled, immediately firing off punches, knocking a couple of rioters to the ground. He and Adriana climbed over the people in their path to reach their friend.

A young man approached Cason's limp body and tried to rip his firearm from his holster.

"Get the fuck back!" commanded a supervisor in a white shirt.

"That's discourtesy. I want your name and badge number!" demanded the anarchist.

"Oh, that's discourtesy? Fuck off! Lt. Cintron, no shield number, motherfucker!" the white shirt responded, pulling his weapon out at the angry wolf pack.

"Hands up. Don't shoot! Black lives matter!" the man chanted.

"I know you rehearsed that, you privileged little punk!" exclaimed the lieutenant. "Test me, Antifa, and I'll bring a whole new meaning to the term, 'white guilt.' Put your hands behind your back before I hurt you."

Officers lifted Cason's body out of harm's way while rookies handcuffed the perpetrators. As they were loading Cason into a police van, he momentarily opened his eyes.

"He's awake!" Adriana yelled as officers began to transport Cason to a nearby hospital.

Jaxton and Adriana couldn't break the human wall that stood before them. They could only watch their friend, injured and at the lowest point of his career, carried away in the middle of a battle for Midtown. The rioters would capture the block then demolish the Macy's windows en route to helping themselves to the designer merchandise inside. The reinforcements came, catching looters on the first floor and making them pay a steep price for their crimes. They punched and kicked officers before a sea of NYPD blue turned the first floor of Macy's into a river of red.

"Stop resisting! Stop resisting!" officers ordered as the sound of batons getting introduced to bones could be heard throughout the fragrance section. When it was all over, one hundred arrests were made by members of the department. All were processed as burglary arrests except one. The man who knocked Cason unconscious with a brick was charged with attempted murder. He would be arraigned on Monday and released due to the disastrous Bail Reform bill.

Jaxton and Adriana held one another and took in the gory spectacle, which would forever be seared into their collective consciousness. The blood of both cops and robbers splattered all over the merchandise counters. The entire night was pretty much soaked in sanguine, and the cursed year underwent its truest test in the heated beakers of the urban crucible. The pair sought to learn where Cason was headed. They hoped that a reunion between them, years later, could still produce a joyful ending. They searched their phones for the nearest hospital.

CHAPTER 8

Eloise's French Kitchen

"Do you want to know how this day started for me?" a distressed Jaxton asked Adriana as they rode a straining MTA bus to Mount Sinai Hospital.

"Fire away. My day started at a yoga class, so yours had to be more excit—"

"It started with me trying to kill myself."

"Like . . . beating yourself up for something you did?"

"No. I literally started the day hanging off the side of the George Washington," he stated, his head dropping, heavy from the shame. "Cason yanked me off the bridge."

"Suicide? So we are talking about *suicide* here? I know I'm not dumb. I just can't see how someone like you—"

"Someone like me?" he asked indignantly.

"What I mean is someone so talented and seemingly happy, with a true zest for life. When we were dating, I thought you were . . . just like . . . indestructible. Nothing ever flustered you. You were unflappable."

"Even so-called unflappable people break down. I know I'm not that—I have delusions but not about that. But even someone who is unflappable has a breaking point. Even they can slip into a place of darkness," he explained.

"What's are the circumstances that caused you to slip into darkness?"

"It's not really that simple. It's more abstract. But if you're looking for logical root causes, I can list those too. I got let go from the magazine. My wife and I keep having these explosive fights over . . . over I don't even know what. She told me she hated me last night to cap off an entire week of fighting and vicious name-calling. It was war. I've lost so many friends to the pandemic. Just last week, I learned that a good friend—Harold was his name—died from coronavirus. This guy was like a jolt of electricity in a human vessel, just a gold-toothed grin with this sharp wit and charisma. I miss him. I never got to say goodbye, and I couldn't even attend his funeral. The city I know . . . the city I love has been absolutely annihilated by the pandemic. All of this takes a toll on a man. It turns you into someone you're not."

"And Cason saved you?"

"He pulled me off the ledge. He literally interrupted me mid-act. He even pulled his gun on me. I would have jumped."

"I'm pretty sure you wouldn't have," she countered.

"I mean . . . Adriana, come on. I couldn't have gotten much closer. And the screwed-up part is now I'm in better condition than he is. He might be fighting for *his* life."

"And you were fighting for yours. I wish I could have spoken to you. I wish I could have told you, 'They can't tear you down. They can't take away your accomplishments.' You have the most popular magazine column, one which penetrates the consciousness of New Yorkers. You have a best-selling book. You have a beautiful daughter, you have a . . . wife," she finished, her voice trailing off dispiritedly.

"I do have a wife."

"And you kissed me."

"I kissed you," he agreed.

"You cheated on her, Jax."

"I did. Maybe for the million kisses we missed out on, for a chance to turn back the hands of time, for a chance to journey into the past and be transported into the future," he declared in a hyperbole only he could get away with.

"But that future can't include me," she acknowledged.

"That moment will include you forever. It is our commemoration and our culmination all in one."

"And it was exhilarating, I admit. For certain, Jax. But do you think it was the last stop for us?"

"I don't know when it's a stop and when it's moving anymore."

The bus traveled through Central Park, past picturesque gazebos, flowering meadows, and the tree-lined transverse. The two former romantic partners rode by Tavern on the Green where they had enthusiastically downed bubbly and partaken of the dizzying and contagious celebratory rituals that had defined their thriving half decade. The weblike necklace lights were off and not a soul occupied the elegant courtyard where they once sat as two supremely infatuated lovers against New York's post-modern canvas. They passed Strawberry Fields, where they once kissed passionately against the black-and-white "Imagine" mosaic in the John Lennon Memorial. They glided past the majestic Belvedere Castle, illuminated purely by moonlight and veiling itself against the darkness of Central Park's Elms. And they took in the Jacqueline Kennedy Onassis Reservoir reflecting the moon's luminous face as the Ninety-Seventh Street Transverse ushered them to their destination.

It was a tour through their past and the nostalgia of their shared highs. Memories were awakened and sentiments revived as the warmth of their rising body heat and that of the midsummer nocturne coalesced them like two lakes at a campsite. They traveled past the shuttered Godiva Chocolates storefront where they once fed each other salted almond truffles with creamy praline centers. When the natural aphrodisiacs were consumed like the couple's handsome features. When their erogenous yearnings were satisfied in unconventional locales in front of voyeuristic New Yorkers. It was a run that came abruptly and unceremoniously to an end one day—like a stock market crash—but would keep a bookmark in the story of their lives deep into their twilight. This was the victory lap they never got amid the emotion of their common companion's physical imperilment. The bus stopped in front of Mount Sinai Hospital, and they rushed in to see Cason, an avenging angel from New York's suddenly battered anti-police landscape.

Jaxton took in the hospital's façade before entering through the pavilion and into a skylit plaza. He pulled Adriana with him as her feet hustled to keep up with his pace. He sprinted and would remember running in with the same intensity ahead of the birth of his beloved, Grace. But she was entering the world then and embodied the beauty of new beginnings. Cason was now in a valley of his life and fighting to retain it. The two pushed through the security doors into the emergency room.

"Excuse me! You can't go in there without a mask," a guard violently snapped as he awakened from a nap.

The two grabbed surgical masks from a wall dispenser and ran past a cardiac patient on a hospital bed. They took in the sea of blue uniforms outside of a curtain, and it was obvious that they had arrived at their injured friend.

"Sergeant Sax?" Jaxton asked.

"Hey, back the hell up. Identify yourself," scolded an officer.

"I'm, I'm a friend. He saved my life. We're like brothers. He's my best friend," Jaxton boasted.

"Well, he's in bad shape," informed a tall man in a stark white shirt with the double gold bars of the captain rank on his lapel. "The brick knocked him out. They think he probably suffered a concussion."

The assault on Cason not only left him concussed but it made him famous. Later that night, a short video clip surfaced of a police supervisor pointing his firearm at a rioter. Naturally, that was all the short clip captured and it soon went viral.

"I want that cop's gun and shield!" demanded Mayor Wilhelm from the safety of his press room. "I want that officer relegated to modified duty until a criminal investigation into his actions can be completed. We can't have innocent citizens being menaced by police on our streets."

After a longer clip emerged, of Cason being knocked unconscious by the brick, it was clear why the officer in the white shirt drew his firearm. A rioter had clearly attempted to steal an unresponsive Cason's gun. The lieutenant drew his weapon, and the assaulter scurried away before being taken into custody. The mayor went silent on the matter after that but later criticized the NYPD's handling of what he insisted were "mostly peaceful protests." It was a chorus that would be repeated often even as the number of NYPD officers who were transported to the hospital continued to mount.

In a surreal moment at the hospital, an officer unlocked his cellphone screen to view the video of Cason being assaulted and the aftermath of it. The video had already been viewed over one hundred thousand times. The officer's quickly put the phone away and inquired into the sergeant's prognosis.

Jaxton and Adriana did not see the awful video—they did not have to—as witnessing it in person created a memory that would often replay in their minds. They sought comfort in one another before the charge nurse informed them that their time was up.

"But wait! Is he going to be okay? What is his status? I know he's critical, but is he stable?" Cason pressed. "Can we at least see him?"

"No. No one is allowed in his room. COVID hasn't just magically disappeared, and we're still working on determining his condition. You guys have to leave now. Only the police actively involved can stay. We've got to lower the headcount by at least half. And *you*, Officer. Excuse me. Your mask!" the nurse reminded. "If you want to stay in the ER, you have to wear a face covering. We have some N95s on the wall if you lost yours."

Jaxton and Adriana were forced to exit the emergency room and come to terms with the reality of their friend's weakened form. Jaxton's phone interrupted them.

"Baby?" Waverly greeted softly, keeping her voice down so as not to awaken Grace.

"Oh, I'm back to being baby again?" he asked.

"You will always be my baby. You just have to be kinder to me," she advised.

"Kinder than what? Actually, hold that thought. You won't believe what happened," Jaxton started.

"You ran into an ex-girlfriend?" she kidded.

"Ex-girlfriend? Where did that come from?"

"Sssh, it was a joke," she replied. "Tell me what actually happened, Jax."

"Cason got attacked with a brick."

"What the hell? What kind of protest is that?"

"A group of anarchists attacked him and his cops. It was a freaking melee. They were armed with other weapons too."

"That's absolutely terrible. I'm sorry to hear that, but it's late, and it sounds like it's dangerous out there. Can you come home now? Grace hasn't seen you today and I'm starting to get worried."

"Didn't you hear what I said? Cason is *seriously* injured. Plus, you told me you hated me. You called me all types of names. You said that you wanted to divorce me," he reminded.

"Well, Jax, people say things when they're mad," she explained. "And what are you going to do? Stay out forever? You have a daughter, and it was a comment made from anger."

"Oh, so that was all just out of anger? I guess that's supposed to minimize it. I won't even tell you the damage that words can do to someone. And I know I have a daughter. Grace is all I keep thinking about."

"Look. We've gone through some tough times lately. Everybody has. But tough times make strong people—"

"And strong people make good times. I know, I know," he completed skeptically.

"We'll get through this," she stated calmly. "Are you coming home?"

"I'll be home as soon as I can. I just have to do one last thing."

"And what's that? . . . Jaxton? . . . Hello?"

Jaxton abruptly hung up, and Adriana, patiently waiting, offered a slight cough as a polite reminder that she was still standing there.

"I know she's your wife. I'm not mad."

"You can't be mad."

"I can be mad. I can absolutely be mad. But I'm not," Adriana explained.

"Well . . . *I'm* mad. Marriage is not everything it's cracked . . . It's challenging—Hey, do you want to go get a coffee?" he asked, interrupting himself.

"That's random. Is anything even open?"

"Well, I know a woman—"

"*You* know a woman, Jax? Surprise."

"who owns a French bakery, smartass."

"And it's open now?" she questioned. "Hello, coronavirus. And have you looked at the time?"

"Time is a construct. She lives right above her shop. I can buzz her," he assured. "She never sleeps. She lives alone. She's like a cat woman without the cats."

The two made their way to Lexington Avenue and East One-Hundredth Street to a small shop called Eloise's French Kitchen. Jaxton looked up at the fire escape where a familiar potted plant and partially opened window gave away his friend's apartment. He repeatedly pressed the button to the intercom. After a few minutes, a petite young lady in a red headscarf emerged, giving Jaxton a kiss on each cheek and snobbishly inspecting Adriana.

"You knew it was me?" Jaxton asked.

"No. I'm expecting an Amazon package. Who the hell else would ring my doorbell at this time? You're lucky I owe you, Jax," the young baker scolded as she opened the door to her croissant shop.

"How much business did my column about you generate again? 'Best spot on the East side'," he reminded.

"Yeah, yeah. You should have said, 'Best spot on any side.' And who is she? I don't recall your wife having eyes like those," Eloise stated before hitting the start button on a coffeemaker.

"My name is Adriana. I'm a friend," she downplayed.

"Well, friend, I'm leaving the key on this counter right here. You can see the coffee is already brewing. I assume you still love it light and sweet?" she turned and asked Jaxton.

"Just like you," he complimented.

"Oh, please, Jax. Cut it out," she dismissed, before shooting Adriana an unpleasant look. Jaxton whispered into Eloise's ear, informing her of what had happened to Cason. She put her hand over her mouth in disbelief and exited to the sound of the bells chiming above the door.

"Another ex-girlfriend?" Adriana asked.

"We had a close, intimate . . . thing," he confessed.

"I'm sure it was light and sweet, right?"

The main counter housed buttery croissants, meringue-based macarons, cream-filled eclairs, and sugary madeleines. The couple reached for the chouquettes, sprinkled with pearl sugar, and took in the small portion of dough.

They sat at a quaint table; the place somehow romantically lit as nutlike coffee aroma wafted through the small space. The air was sweet and delicate, sugary, and smoky. It seemed to enhance the experience. They each sipped cautiously as the coffees were still hot.

"Mmm, delicious," Adriana praised.

"We needed this. This respite."

"Did you ever sleep with her?"

"Okay, that was forward. Um . . . no—yes. There wasn't much sleeping going on. We dated intensely you could say."

"Intensely?" she replied with distrust. "What's that a euphemism for?"

"For intensely. What made you want to come out here and protest?" He quickly shifted the topic.

"I mean I think it's terrible that innocent black people keep getting murdered by police."

"It's a tragedy anytime someone dies at the hands of police. But innocent?" he challenged. "I'm not sure if being arrested for sexual assault qualifies as innocent."

"Well, not innocent in that sense. But cops can't be judge, jury, and executioner, right? Innocent until proven guilty in this country still, no? There's a legal process in place."

"Sure. And the cop is innocent until proven guilty too. But I just feel that if you're high on drugs, committing a crime, and resisting arrest, you might be placing yourself in a position to be harmed by police officers," he said, pushing back. "They are human beings, and they get scared too."

"Yeah, but you don't deserve to die just for resisting arrest," she rebutted.

"No one deserves to die. But I don't think you should make officers feel afraid of not going home to their families, which might push their actions toward violence," he countered, elevating in tone.

"Police officers are trained to deescalate, not to go up in volume. They're supposed to calm people down."

"How do you calm someone down when they're high on drugs and physically violent? Do you deploy the 'hug a thug' method?"

"Crisis intervention techniques, empathetic communication, and compassion," she argued.

"Compassion? Did you *not* see our friend knocked the fuck out with a cinder block?"

"It was a brick," she corrected.

"Oh, okay," he replied, pantomiming pulling out his hair. "I guess that doesn't hurt as much so it's really no big deal, right? Let's all go home then."

"Why are you yelling?"

"Because you are totally ignoring the fact that irate, high-on-drugs, violent people don't want to comply with officers' orders. They want to hurt the officer so they can get away," he went on, slamming his hand on the booth and spilling some of his café au lait.

"Calm the hell down, Jax! We're trying to have a civil conversation!"

"I'm trying to be civil, but what you're proposing is ludicrous."

"Let me ask you a question. Do you believe that black lives matter?"

"Here we go again with this! *Absolutely.* Is that really even a legitimate question? Black lives are instrumental, vital, *crucial* in this country. You would be hard-pressed to find an individual who would say, 'No, black lives don't matter.' But I reject the notion that every time a black person dies at the hands of police in this country, it is because of his race and that of the police officer. Race is not the reason for everything or every outcome in police-involved deaths. It is usually criminality and resisting arrest. That is the nexus. But that would require accountability, which seems to be taboo right now."

"Well, that's what white privilege is. You don't experience life through the same lens that black people do, so you can't fully comprehend their fear," she explained.

"I'd be afraid too if I were breaking the law. If I were black and law-abiding, I wouldn't fear anything," he asserted.

"White privilege."

"These bullshit terms! No. I'd fear my neighbors because black-on-black crime is the biggest threat to black people in America today and I have statistics, not anecdotes, to prove it," he argued.

"Crime is intra-racial."

"So is ignorance evidently."

"Racist! You are a goddamn racist," she accused.

"Typical. That's the thing about you liberals. Every time someone says anything you don't agree with, you see fit to call that person a racist or a bigot or a homophobe or some other stigmatizing term. We list facts. You dismiss it as racist. We list stats, you say, 'Math is racist,' and say we're using it to taint an entire population. You guys are emotional, fragile, simple-minded, and confused and I don't mind excoriating you every now and then because, quite frankly, you guys deserve it."

"You think *I'm* confused?"

"Oh, that's what you got from that?" he replied, feigning laughter. "Well, I dated you for a good while, so I *know* you're confused."

"Oh, screw you, asshole!" she shot, lobbing a French pastry directly onto his face.

A sugar puff stuck to his cheek as his eyes widened. He brushed the white flakes with his finger and brought them into his mouth.

"Sweet like any good liberal cream puff. When dialogue fails, violence ensues," he stated pointedly.

"Don't call me a cream puff!"

"Cannoli!"

"You asshole!"

"Profiterole."

"You are pushing me! You want to see violence? I'll show you violence," she stated, biting down on her lower lip and seductively sizing up Jaxton.

As the two stared heatedly at one another, something usually only experienced in nighttime fantasies unfurled almost cosmically.

Adriana reached across the table, grabbing his face and pulling it toward her. She kissed his mouth and slid her tongue across the spot on his cheek containing the sugary residue. He ripped open her shirt, slightly tearing the fabric surrounding the buttonholes, exposing supple breasts. She lowered her bra, dipped her nipple in his coffee cup, and guided the conical part of her breast into his mouth as he savored the foamy taste. She grabbed a tarte aux framboise and stuffed it in his mouth while consuming a tarte aux myrtilles herself.

"*Mmm*, fucking delicious," she released.

They kissed over the essences of fusing berry flavors, and she slid a chocolate religieuse down her panties. He pushed the table out of the way and dropped to his knees in front of her seat, consuming choux pastry from within her thighs. Piped buttercream frosting leaked from the dough pieces and delighted his tongue as he tasted ganache and subtle hints of her natural cream in the same mouthful. She quivered in her seat, legs pointing in separate directions as he submissively satisfied her from an obedient position. She climaxed, squeezing raspberries covered in powdered sugar in one hand and ripe blueberries in the other. Bright red and deep purple exuded from her clenched fists as she lightly trembled in post-coital bliss. He came up from her dessert-covered loins and kissed her again. She painted his features in what was now berry preserves, giving him an impromptu war paint on each side of his face.

He stood up, calmly sipped his coffee, and noted through heavy breaths, "We probably have to clean this mess up before Eloise gets back."

"Well, what about you?" she asked.

"That was my climax," he replied.

"But you didn't—"

"No, I'm fine. I um . . . I can finish myself off or something."

"Or your wife can," she stated stingingly.

"I thought we were done with that. I just crossed every single line that exists for you."

"How very sacrificial of you, Jaxton Bello. Let me see. She got the diamond ring" she started, trying to regain her breath, "the gorgeous wedding ceremony, the baby, the house in Westchester. Basically, the entire American Dream. And I got fucked, literally!"

"Well, you just got an orgasm."

"Fuck the orgasm, asshole. I can get that by myself. I wanted more."

"Well, things aren't always exactly as they seem. I mean I'm blessed. My daughter is precious. She's perfect, but . . ."

"I'm sure she is. It's just that she should have been *our* daughter," she cited painfully.

Jaxton approached her slowly and threw both of his arms around her shoulders. He pulled her lovingly into his chest and cradled her there. He palmed the back of her head as her hair flowed evenly between his fingers. He kissed her forehead with real love behind it. The embrace was long and meaningful, and the unlikely culmination of a relationship forged in a bar and concluded in a French bakery. The two tidied up the mess they made, and each grabbed a chocolate croissant as they exited. They stared at one another outside the bakery as a sneaky wind blew the Eloise's French Kitchen sign around and the moon lit up the awning, practically the only illuminated object in the entire street.

"Was this my last night with you?" she asked vulnerably.

"Was this your last night with me?"

"Was this the last time we . . . you and I . . .," she attempted to say before choking up.

"I don't know for sure, but I think this is possibly . . . It's quite likely this could be our last chapter," he surmised like swinging a bat at a knuckleball.

"So that right there is the last memory we'll ever share?"

"It could be the last *new* memory we ever . . . um, we ever forge together . . .," he mumbled.

Jaxton took her by the hand and walked her away from the bakery door. It was as if her heart was left there by the door like old newspapers and other recyclables. Jaxton pulled the door behind him, locking it with the single key attached to a pink cupcake keychain charm. They left behind a seemingly whimsical place, outside the parameters of reality with confectioners' sugar puffing in the air and their endmost memory hovering sweetly there as well.

"Can you hold me one last time?" she asked. "Not like a friend. Hug me like a wife."

The air had momentarily turned crisp, and the moment was proportionally cold.

"This is hard," he understated.

"The way that this experience ends will literally shape my ability to ever love again," she stated.

"No pressure though, right?" he awkwardly deadpanned.

He could read in her eyes how much this moment weighed to her. He did not know how to properly proceed, how to disengage without shattering her.

"What did she give you that I didn't?"

"It's not about that. Sometimes love lasts and sometimes it doesn't. It's elusive like that. Sometimes it comes back around once it's too late, and sometimes everything just lines up perfectly," he explained.

"Do you think I'll ever find someone like you out there again?" she asked.

"I hope not," he replied. "I know it's selfish of me."

"Why does goodbye not seem authentic right now?"

"Because you remember the magic of our first meeting?"

"I remember your bullshit line about destiny. Do you remember the reason why you left me?" she asked, attempting to awaken old ghosts, "I know there is no tomorrow for us, but I just want to—"

"Look. Don't get me wrong. I loved you. I loved you deeply. I saw the future in your flawless face and nothing less. I did see you as my destiny."

"You were the only man whose touch I ever wanted to feel," she poured out with ardor and pent-up anger. "Is this my great love lesson? Is this supposed to be what I take with me to my next relationship? To make me better somehow?"

"I'm sorry," Jaxton confessed. "I'm sorry I wasn't—Look. We were young," he offered. "Maturity matters too."

"We were mature enough. We just didn't know it. I wish we could turn back time."

"I do too," he admitted, "but I can't have one foot in the past and one in the future."

Adriana searched for answers that the night could not possibly be long enough to reveal. Jaxton held her the way a protagonist holds the female lead in a movie. The moment was almost as cinematic as it was heartbreaking. It was extended but had an expiration on it like a gas station pump meter. They would decouple but painfully.

Jaxton watched Adriana walk away for the final time and sought to organize the inconceivable events of the day in his disarranged mind. He reflected and was suddenly tired.

"I'm going to send you the bill," Eloise surprised him, appearing as if out of thin air. "And didn't you marry another chick?"

"Yes. You're very observant, Eloise. Thank you for accommodating us."

"I said I'm going to send you the bill. I'll take inventory in the morning," she reiterated.

"I might owe you a table too. I think it's uh . . . Never mind. I'll send you the money in the a.m. How are you still open? I thought everything was closed due to COVID-19."

"You think I'm going to let my business go bankrupt, waiting on the government for a bullshit stimulus check? Black market brioche, baby. People make appointments, I deliver the bread," she said with a wink.

"You sure do. You've always come through for me," Jaxton credited.

"Jaxton?"

"Eloise?"

"Go home to your family. There's nothing left for you to do tonight."

"I still have to see Cason," he reminded. "He saved my life. I can't leave him at the hospital like that."

"You've always loved that man."

"He's my brother."

Jaxton was, once again, unaccompanied. He peered out at a city that was collapsing into ruins after having charted so much of it on this most unforgettable day. He reflected on how the pandemic hit and, overnight, so much of New York was wood-shuttered. Yellow and purple school bulletin boards with Easter bunnies and baskets would remain unchanged, displaying out-of-season themes. Restaurants were unoccupied with place settings still set, glasses upside down, napkin rings holding an unused cloth, and nary an aroma of any decipherable cuisine in the air. Office buildings were empty as "working remotely" emerged as a phrase that would become ubiquitous in the vernacular of "Zoom meeting" zombies. Retail stores were as static as the faceless mannequins in the window. Sidewalks, once the great racetrack of urban civilization, were no longer sprinted on by the masses. The rhythm and momentum of New York's gravity had finally been interrupted.

You could see the cracks in the pavement, the imperfections, and the perfect ravages of time—the unrepaired depletions, the natural erosion, the depreciation of the incomparable beauty that so often saw its profile plastered on the American magazine. The lack of humankind stepping on the spot-lit stage exposed New York's age and neglect. Void of any inhabitants, New York's personality had been stolen by a virus whose mysterious origins were as misunderstood as its effect. The city was a barren landscape, and it would be flooded like a town whose dam had burst, leading to a sudden, rapid, uncontrolled release of human voices and emotions.

COVID had crippled the city, and the demonstrators had badly brutalized it while it was down. The aftermath of lost jobs; sheltering in place; the absence of sports and entertainment as a diversion; the relentless political finger-pointing; and the privilege of being able to wake up, assemble, destroy property, and face no serious legal consequences would manifest in various unsightly ways for months to come. This was evident, most notably, in a hellacious crime wave that would sweep through New York, as well as some of the most iconic American cities. Seattle, Minneapolis, Washington DC, and Portland were among the cities that would witness violent protests coupled with the senseless loss of life. And to top everything off, there was a presidential election coming up in November. It would be the most consequential election since the election of 1964, held amid the transformative civil rights movement.

Jaxton would have to process all that had transpired on that day and proceed with his life with a new sensibility. All new considerations had to be made with race relations, relationships with police, and equity and inclusion in mind. Once the voice of New York, Jaxton had to listen more and imagine life in the shoes of the marginalized to understand where New York was headed. The fate of the city was being written, and the stage had been set for a complex and troubling period. A shift in power was occurring, and Democratic politicians were on board. The forces of change were unleashed, and they traded their ethics for votes by not condemning the violence that accompanied it.

Jaxton had to advance against a new terrain that appeared more like a minefield and less like a municipal street. And if he were truly a microcosm for New York, survival and reinvention would be sterling prerequisites for the operative comparison and subsequent rebirth. Jaxton took a moment to memorialize this, typing frenziedly into his phone:

> Hardly any light was visible, and as I peered out at Lower Manhattan, I spied on a voyeuristic city on anesthesia after a frenetic, decades-long run to the top. The island that once flowered and unfurled like a trumpet lily was static and poised to pass the torch to some other

budding metropolis. The buildings that had exchanged those early morning whispers and inspired human dreams as distant as the sun stood as vacant party venues with undelivered invitations. As the sun was preparing to rise on a dawn that I didn't think I'd live to see, the curtains were coming down on the wildest act of the Broadway play that is my life and the macrocosmic city in which it flourished. These were strange times and growing stranger still. And the strangest thing is no one could write the ending because no one foresaw the beginning.

CHAPTER 9

Birth and Rebirth

Jaxton's thoughts floated him back to the birth of his daughter and a reflection on how that event changed his composition. Her delivery was laborious and operatic. A doctor had entered the room during the dusk and explained certain procedures to him and his wife.

"I'm just checking in. Everything is normal, relatively speaking, currently. If you see a bunch of doctors enter the room and their eyes are like this," she said, pantomiming eyes as wide open as saucers, "then you know things took a turn . . . a turn for the worse," she finished with a smile incongruous with the information presented.

Jaxton remembered feeling like a trainer in a corner of a boxing ring. He would give mindful instruction to Waverly, rooted in knowledge and insight extracted from the pregnancy books he had consumed in preparation for this.

"Slow deep breaths, my love. Control your breathing," he would remind her gently. "Visualize our beautiful princess being born."

Waverly smiled but recognized that she had a marathon ahead of her. The epidural had been administered and was coursing through her spine. She was accustomed to being the focal point, but not in this way, with expectations of delivering at a finish line. She usually shrunk against pressure but was now the center of all activity at room 1013 in Mt. Sinai Hospital. In police radio code, 1013 was a numeric representation of "officer in distress." It would now forever be the birthplace of Grace Adeline Bello, Gracie, they would sometimes call her.

———

Jaxton kept his eye skeptically affixed to the heart rate monitor. The jagged lines; the blood pressure; and oxygen saturation, respiration, and temperature were all memorized vital signs with levels to sustain. Jaxton focused on the screens and attempted to grasp what the best metrics were for each. Watching the multicolored lines could almost hypnotize a person. Jaxton stood, completely engaged, when 160 abruptly became 120, and 120 suddenly dipped to 80. Grace was not tolerating labor well and Jaxton scanned around the room for someone to explain why the numbers had declined so drastically.

"Excuse me, nurse! What's going on with the monitor?"

Eighty quickly became 60 and then rapidly dropped to 20.

"Paging doctor Smoke! Paging Doctor Smoke! To room 1013 immediately!" a nurse transmitted.

Doctors and nurses of all different color scrubs poured into the room. Waverly's eyes expanded to their corneal limits. An oxygen mask was forced on her and she stared blankly into Jaxton's eyes, which were bulging with consternation. He locked back in on the heart rate, whose number had dropped to 10 and then 8 and finally a blinking yellow question mark that felt like a concluding liver punch. Grace was in total distress, and the ancillary staff prepared a room for an emergency C-section or worse.

"Please, God. Please, God," Jaxton repeated, praying that the punctuation mark would again take the form of a triple-digit number.

He dropped to his knees, fingers intertwined, as he took in the trauma from a shoelace level. Jaxton begged and he cried. He forced his will upon his prayer, trying to sway God from making Grace another casualty of neonatal death. He marshaled every ounce of emotion he possessed to alter the readings displayed on the monitor. Jaxton began to mentally prepare to hear from doctors that Grace had died.

And then, suddenly, the question mark morphed to an 8, and the 8 transformed to a 20 before steadily rising in increments of ten. Waverly had no idea how close Grace came to dying on that cloudy morning at Mt. Sinai Hospital. As the heart rate climbed to 120 beats per minute, Jaxton's tears gave way to a smile, like sunlight pushing through nimbus cloud cover. He held his wife's hand as she was urged by doctors to push and breathe. They could almost see Grace; they reached for her. She was nearly there.

Jaxton counted with his wife, slowly to ten, as each push got stronger and closer to delivering Grace into the world. As he squeezed support into her hand, a tuft of dark brown hair emerged, crowning gloriously and altering Jaxton's heartbeat. The cadence of his count was interrupted by spells of emotions. He pulled himself together to complete ten full counts to the number 10. Waverly, the vessel delivering Grace into this new realm, looked focused, if disoriented, but poised to become a mother.

"You're doing amazing, just keep going, my love," he guided in a cracking voice.

"One . . . two . . . three . . ." he urged, eyeing a meeting with his daughter, an extraterrestrial arriving in her new world.

He would soon meet her, which is a way of saying he would soon be introduced to his purpose. He was tremendously humbled by it. It would bring him crashing to his knees in a way that nothing else could.

The final push propelled Grace into this world, one arm extended and her fist balled up, into the clutches of waiting doctors. Waverly bled tears from the corners of her eyes that streamed down her face like rivulets from marshy hills. Jaxton stalked the doctors to a station where antibiotic eye ointments are administered. He requested to carry the most precious thing that he would ever hold. He was amazed by her featherlike weight and how quickly she curled into him as he put his cheek against her little newborn ear. It seemed like they had met in heaven before this earth. Waverly delivered her placenta and received Grace for breastfeeding. Grace instantly latched and consumed the nourishment of the colostrum from Waverly's swollen mammary glands. The secretion gave Grace the antibodies she would need for the upcoming familial hospital visits. Jaxton again went down to his knees and erupted with emotion. His tears puddled on the hospital tile as he sobbed and came to terms with the new, magnificent life that he had just been gifted on the tenth floor of Mt. Sinai Hospital. It was room number thirteen. Officer in distress. He would always love and hate that number concurrently.

"Children will bring you to your knees," he recalled a friend telling him years ago.

These words resounded deafeningly as he was one with the delivery room floor, speaking to God in his internal voice.

"Thank you, thank you," he barely sounded, his fingers again clenched in invocation. God had enabled Waverly to deliver a life-completing little girl into their lives.

"You did it," Jaxton congratulated.

"I did it for you," Waverly said, barely audible. "I know how badly you wanted a daughter. Always come home to her."

As Jaxton reminisced on this unsurpassed moment, the love that he felt for his young daughter and his wife began to, more powerfully and gravitationally, pull him home. He was taken by immense guilt about his infidelity with Adriana and he wanted to return to the household and his family to rebuild. He opened an e-mail reply on his phone that he had composed during his intense courtship with Waverly. It read:

> I awoke in the middle of the night with joy dancing in my heart as you invaded my unguarded mind. I recited a prayer, in hopes that we would collide in person soon before I dove back into the realm of dream to draw you there with me. I'm ecstatic my e-mail made you smile. From what shines through in photos, you have a luminous one and so I'm convinced the room where your meeting was held turned incandescent. Your smile has tons of watts in it—and that's the type of light this world is starving for. You seem so grounded and strike me as a precious stone of a person. And since diamonds are forever that's the one I'm describing. I reciprocate your "muahs" (not so sure if guys are permitted to write muah) and I'll take your X's and O's and translate them into the real hugs and kisses I vow to blanket you in. We can change the sky together, you and me. Are we meeting soon? Seems like we already have, in heaven before this earth.

His own words smacked Jaxton across the face. He recalled the supernatural love that enveloped his honeymoon period with Waverly. He ached to see her again, but he had to ensure that the friend who made it possible by saving his life could see his sweetheart again too.

With the end goal of concluding the odyssey and returning home to Westchester, Jaxton began to make his way back to the hospital to rejoin his injured brethren. On his way there, he crashed confoundingly into an old friend thought to have succumbed to the coronavirus, while racing down Fifth Avenue.

"Harold? Harold! Is that you?" he asked, both men illuminated by an old-fashioned cast-iron Deskey twin lamppost.

An older, African American male in gold-rimmed spectacles and a white goatee turned toward Jaxton.

"No, fool. It's not me. It's your momma. What kind of dumbass question is that? You don't trust your own eyes? You want to borrow my seventy-six-year-old light browns instead?"

"Harold, Gabriel told me you got coronavirus and—"

"And what? Come on, fool! Wear a mask, wash your hands, and keep your distance. If you can't follow three easy steps, I don't know what to say to you. Now back the hell up," Harold stated with a slight beat to it.

"There's only one, Harold," Jaxton commented, hugging his senior pal. "I see you still haven't lost anything off your fastball."

"Fastball? M'uhfucka, that was my off-speed pitch. You wanna see a fastball, gimme a real batter to throw it to. You about a .200 hitta, and I'm bein' generous," the male kidded. "Now stop hugging me. Six feet, fool. I told you I swing, but I don't swing that way."

"You always have jokes. It's about two in the morning. What the heck are you doing out?"

"What are you, my fatha? Did I come from yo nut sack? I don't need to tell you nothin' 'bout what I'm doin'. You gotta answer to your wife about what the hell it is you doin' out here?" he flipped. "Where is your lady friend?"

"My lady friend?" Jaxton asked.

"Nigga, did I stutter? I know you ain't workin', so what the hell is you doin' out if you ain't out wit' ya side piece?"

"Come on, Harold," Jaxton replied with guilt in his heart.

"Don't 'Come on, Harold' me. You oughta be getting in yo own ass for sneakin' around like a damn thief in the night. Back in my day, I woulda collared yo ass just for bein' out at this time," he informed before letting out an amused laugh. The two men held one another, and Jaxton again squeezed his friend and gripped the plaid fabric around the shoulder pads of his well-worn blazer.

"Why did Gabby tell me you passed away? I was heartbroken by that. I couldn't sleep. I love you, man."

"You don't love shit," Harold rejected. "You don't know how to love."

"I do, Harold."

"Right. Mr. Cupid himself. How's Waverly?" he asked through a smile adorned with sparkling gold dental bridges.

"She's home with Grace. I'm trying to get back home to them. It's been a hell of a day. I just have to make sure Cason is okay first."

"Cason? I just finished seeing that nigga'."

"You got the video too? Damn. That thing traveled fast."

"Video? My man, is you high on crack? I just saw that nigga come out of Mount Sinai Hospital with a whole bunch of us. I say *us*, but you ain't one of us. Don't think that because you did a couple a ride-along, you a cop," Harold stated. "You ain't no damn cop. You gotta earn this shit."

"I know. I know that, Harold. But Cason was admitted to Mount Sinai," Jaxton replied.

"My man, I told you I was seventy-six. Did I tell you I suffer from dementia or some shit? Cason walked out of Mount Sinai Hospital. I know because I gave him a goddam' pound and because I'm still sane. Unlike yo ass. Thinking a nigga is dead and shit."

"So he walked out? Like on his feet?" Jaxton asked.

"No, on his balls. Is you fuckin' drunk? I saw him stroll out. Then he jumped into a police van. I don't understand where the confusion is coming from."

"Harold, I saw him get hit with a brick. He got knocked out by a Black Lives Matter protester—"

"Well, he must have had his helmet on."

"Thank God, he did."

"Okay then. You know I know that shit protects yo ass from everything," Harold said.

"It's just that he looked . . . out of it. I can't believe he walked out."

"You know that muhfucka tough as hell. He was down at 911, saving muhfuckas. You think a brick is gon do him in? A goddam' Twin Tower fell on his ass, and he walked outta there wearin' debris, lookin' like a goddam ghost. A brick ain't gonna do nothin' to a nigga like that. He wears that 911 shit like a force field."

Jaxton had never considered how the effects of witnessing human beings leap out of windows at the World Trade Center and having the South Tower fall on him as he stood on Liberty Street had shaped and fortified Cason. He was a sentinel then, standing amidst building-size billows of smoke. The heat that was released, the chaos on a mathematical scale, the concentrated carnage that plummeted downward was inconceivably absorbed by Cason as he stood his ground. Somehow, he walked away from it. So many were obliterated on that day, but Cason was bolstered. His self-efficacy was given steroids after surviving the greatest human tragedy of the modern era. Half a million tons shook seismic instruments, but Cason walked out of it in work boots. It should have been no surprise that he ripped the intravenous needle out of his arm and relied on his own two feet to stride out of Mount Sinai Hospital with his chin in the air. It was, in fact, accurate that Cason walked out of the emergency room and into the next battlefield of his life.

"Did he say he was going home?"

"Hell no. He was going to Rockefeller Center," Harold said in defiance.

"Rockefeller Center is closed," Jaxton remarked.

"I don't think looters care," Harold said with a laugh.

"I guess I know where I have to go then."

"You better get there," Harold encouraged. "Start walkin' 'cause I ain't paying for yo Uber."

Jaxton nodded in agreement. He faced southbound and was about to begin the final stretch before quizzically turning to Harold.

"Harold . . .," he called as the friends looked into each other's faded eyes. "What were you actually doing down here?"

"I was attendin' the Black Lives Matter protest."

"BLM? Are you pro-cop or are you anti-cop? Make up your mind, man."

"I'm for cops, and I'm for black lives. Is that a fuckin' problem? I'm a black man who served twenty-seven years with the police department. You tryna check my credentials?" Harold shot back. "You tryna check me, nigga? You can't check me until you walk a mile in my shoes and then walk my beat as a cop. You ain't done neither. All you do is write about it wit' yo silly-ass computer bag, so all you doin' now is talkin' shit."

"You're right . . . I'm just trying to find my friend. I'm sorry, Harold."

"Don't be sorry. Be good. Find his ass. And make sure he goes hard on these anarchists. They're tryna burn this shit down. You know what he gotta do right?"

"No," Jaxton returned feebly.

"The next time one of them raises a brick to him, he gotta light they ass up. Tell our boy I said, 'I rather be judged by twelve than carried by six.' You copy? . . . I said did you copy, nigga?"

"I copy," Jaxton answered. "Loud and clear."

"Okay then. Now get yo ass movin'."

A mentally exhausted Jaxton turned his head south and then gazed back toward the corner, and Harold was no more. He sought to track his pal as he walked away, but there was no remaining evidence of him. The space where Harold and he conversed was oddly illuminated by an uncanny glow.

Jaxton was disoriented, but he traveled the mile and a half to where he believed Cason would be. He could hear the commotion the closer he got to Fifty-Seventh Street where the UNICEF Snowflake is raised to sparkle each Christmas. As he approached the shopping district, he could hear the unmistakable sound of glass shattering. Police vehicles streaked down the avenue, ready to engage with the disorderly demonstrators. Jaxton moved along briskly, looking to cover the momentous event in real time and reunite with his resurrected friend for one last triumph.

CHAPTER 10

Battle for New York

Bergdorf Goodman, Louis Vuitton, Chanel, Prada, Gucci, Valentino, Versace, Dolce and Gabbana, and Sephora lined the luxurious Fifth Avenue like a red-carpet procession normally seen on the backs of Hollywood luminaries. The most opulent stretch of retail anywhere in the United States except perhaps for Rodeo Drive cut through the main artery of New York like a diamond-encrusted catheter extracting currency from enthusiastic purchasers. The number of dollars contained there represented American consumerism and capitalistic might in a way not witnessed at any other address of the city. The cultured preeminence of Great New York was encapsulated by ostentatious storefronts. American Renaissance mansions, Vanderbilt edifices, French Renaissance, and Gothic-style palaces now housed gaudy designer brands coveted by all fashion-conscious hearts. Limestone facades, French stones, and other emblems of riches gave way to futuristic twenty-first-century shine. Gold, glitter, and gaud illuminated this canyon during the day but were loudly muted at night. But now, the blaring bash of burglaries was the predominant sound that reverberated in the balmy New York air.

The moment seemed to hearken back to the turn of the century when New York emerged as two oddly paradoxical cities, breathtakingly diverse and cosmopolitan yet surprisingly impudent and closed off. It was as if the city capitalists wagered that they could gather all the world's people and riches at one address without getting entangled in its profound conflicts and differences. Back in 2001, it was held almost subversively that we could enjoy the financial fruits of globalization while being separated from its perils. As money came in from around the world, so too did envy, hatred, and industrial violence on a biblical scale. This culminated in commercial airlines being used as jackknives and monuments to the clouds being leveled down to their bedrock. New York's four-hundred-year march to the center of the world was commemorated by the titanic wreckage of the World Trade Center.

In 2013, twelve years of rebuilding the most transcendent city on planet Earth was inherited by the race-obsessed mayor, who was obsequious to his politically ambitious wife. He ran in criticism to the broken windows theory and made a vow to make "stop, question, and frisk" obsolete. But now the windows were breaking in real time, and the maligned police department was at a shortage to deal with the barbarity. Glass fracturing became a new, ubiquitous refrain, and the city—previously closed off due to COVID 19—was pried open with crowbars and other burglar's tools and the opposite of distancing was exhibited during the raid.

Jaxton jogged down Fifth Avenue, unsteady cellphone camera in hand, seeking to capture the destruction and contest those who would later repeat that it was a mostly peaceful protest. He was standing on the corner of W. Sixty-First Street when a blue-and-white van abruptly stomped its brakes, leaving skid marks on the street about a quarter of a block long. The van turned violently into the handicap ramp, sending a trash receptacle flying, almost taking out the traffic signal post altogether.

"Jaxton?" the van itself appeared to say before the front passenger door with "Courtesy, professionalism, and respect" on it swung open wildly.

"Yes?" he replied meekly, hands semi-raised, unsure of the intention of the speaker.

"Are you going to jump in or are you fine with watching the city burn from this vantage point?" asked a male with his head wrapped in white bandages, red with blood.

"'Jump in?' Jaxton confusedly asked. "Cason? Holy shit! What the fuck are you doing here? I thought you were—"

"Dead?"

"No, not dead, but in intensive care or something," Jaxton replied. "But then Harold said he saw you."

"Harold? I haven't seen Harold since the lockdown—"

"You sure? He told me he saw—"

"And it's going to take a lot more than a brick to my head to take me out of this fight. They should have fucking shot me," he said with defiance buttressed by ferocious self-efficacy.

"No, they shouldn't have. They shouldn't have laid a finger on you."

"Oh, no? So what are you going to do about it, Rambo?" Cason asked.

Jaxton yanked Cason out of the front passenger seat by the hand and into an embrace.

"How did you know I was going to be on the bridge?" Jaxton questioned.

"Really? Is it interview time again? I'll tell you later after we resolve all this crap. I'm glad we're both right here, right now. How did we get here? Who the hell knows?"

"Sarge, they're destroying the Apple store!" an officer in the van's front seat yelled out.

Jaxton and the sergeant both jumped into the van and the doors banged shut.

"Guys, pass Jax one of the extra riot helmets," Cason ordered as the van sped down Fifth Avenue.

"Boss, we only have nine. There's nine of us, and there are nine riot helmets."

"So let him have one of the ballistic helmets," Cason responded.

"Ballistic helmets?" Jaxton interjected. "Are we expecting bullets to fly?"

"Just make sure you duck. Everybody out of the van!" Cason shouted as Jaxton clumsily put on an NYPD ballistic helmet and flung himself off the van's boarding step.

Eight officers and their supervisor followed and charged directly into the technology company's store to protect its electronics from the bandits attempting to claim them as not negotiated "reparations."

"Police don't move!" an officer futilely yelled as looters exited with boxes of new smartphones and tablets. Cason's crew blockaded the doors, and the sergeant called for reinforcements.

"Central, let me get an 85 to the Apple store on Fifth Avenue and Fifty-Ninth Street! We have numerous burglaries occurring. We need a mobile field force and the Disorder Control Unit. We have multiple collars here, Central!"

The store contained about fifty looters, far outnumbering the weary officers. Many of the thieves found an avenue of egress. At that moment, another wave of looters charged for the doors with their swiped goods, and the squad of cops pulled out their batons and held them in the ready stance. One emboldened robber picked up a chair and swung it against an officer's head, splintering it into pieces and dropping the officer, face first, onto the floor. Jaxton pulled out his cellphone and began to capture the fracas.

"Squad, they're all collars. Every single one of them is a collar. Let's go!" Cason demanded as rioters' punches were countered with officers' shiny black nightsticks. Smartphones were batted out of protesters' hands by polycarbonate cracking upon their knuckles. iPhones in boxes were smacked over display counters and help desks. Officers took punches to their face shields and fought back with pepper spray streams to the perpetrators' eyes. The squad of eight was slowly pushed back. One was incapacitated by the chair shot; one was savagely thrown to the ground; another was kicked in the abdomen, folding over instantly onto his horizontally held staff. The assuring sound of sirens blared, signaling that reinforcements were near. Police rely on solidarity, but something more like saviors were required in this case. The officers, right then outnumbered, grabbed whoever they could and handcuffed them, creating a small line of arrestees in one nook of the store. Objects were thrown at them, but they were still able to effect arrests for burglary and criminal possession of stolen property despite having almost forty perpetrators escaping, unearned goods in tow.

"SRG 2 sergeant, Central. We have ten under here. Can you send me an arrest team and a wagon for transport?"

Reserves arrived and a phalanx of cops staged outside the store, and Cason's crew passed off the defendants to a specialized unit trained in mass arrest processing. The squad regrouped and officers assessed their injuries.

"Is everyone okay?" Cason asked through labored breaths. "Anyone . . . Hold on, guys . . . Shit! . . . Is anybody hurt?"

"Sarge, I got hit over the head with a fucking chair!" replied an officer. "I gotta go LOD."

"You had your helmet on, right?"

"Yeah, Sarge. That's what saved my ass!"

"Okay, so I'll do your line of duty paperwork when we get back to the base," Cason assured.

"I want to get checked out now, Sarge. My head is pounding."

"You will. You will! After we're done here. I can't send you plus one of the guys to guard you at the hospital right now and diminish our personnel. It's all hands on deck."

"Sarge, we're fucking outnumbered! I don't think the department had a plan for this shit. We're dead. We need to tactically retreat, maybe go back to the base and come up with a plan," the officer argued passionately.

"What does that van say? 'Serve and protect,' right? These fucking anarchists are tearing up our city!' Cason exclaimed. "We don't have time to go back and draw up a plan. The plan is we gotta dig deep tonight. We gotta go somewhere. Somewhere we probably haven't been asked to go *ever* in our careers."

"Come on, Sarge," he chimed.

"Don't 'Come on, Sarge' me. You signed up for this. We all did. I'll prepare all the reports you want once we get relieved. But right now, it's us. This is it. The nine of us have to stay together!"

"Um, excuse me . . . am I not standing right here?" Jaxton reminded. "Ten is the number. Someone pass me a spare baton. I'll get busy too."

"Hey, Sarge, you got your very own paparazzi following you, huh?" an officer questioned to a small chorus of laughs.

"Yeah, paparazzi. Sure. That's me. I'm a writer. I'm a journalist. What do you guys call it? Fake news, right?"

"Fake news," an officer parroted.

"I hear you, guys. And if I were you, I wouldn't trust some guy that just showed up at the end either. But I've been writing columns for a decade that truly capture the essence of what it means to be a police officer in this city. This is not my first rodeo or my first ride along . . ."

"Is it your first riot along?" an officer asked, garnering laughs and quips.

"It is my first riot. I guess there's a first for everything. But when I first met your sergeant, he described a procession of bodies jumping out of the windows at the World Trade Center. This guy, who doesn't look like much, I'll admit, was walking through the pile in lower Manhattan, probably with the same worn-out boots he's wearing now. I'm talking about jets and skyscrapers used for evil. Over tangled steel and pulverized glass, above concrete ruins and subterranean fires. Your sergeant was digging for living New Yorkers while most of you were trying to find *Waldo*. September 11 decimated the city—and the country—but it did not decimate the spirit of New York. We fought back. Sergeant Sax fought back! He risked his life and getting cancer and all types of respiratory diseases to look for survivors in the wreckage of a terrorist attack never witnessed in our country. He was a hero, and no one even knew his name. And you know who else he saved? He saved me. When the sun rose this morning, I was hanging off the pedestrian walkway of the George Washington Bridge. I wasn't taking pictures or feeding the pigeons. I was trying to kill myself. I wanted to die!"

The officers were completely frozen by this, ceasing all conversation and focusing singularly on the speaker.

"You never know where life is going to take you. Look, I started the day attempting to commit suicide, and I'm going to end it by pushing back rioters alongside members of the NYPD. My wife probably thinks I'm out with my mistress—that's a whole another story—but my real mistress is New York City. Right here where we stand. Manhattan, I love her. The crown jewel of the country. There are rioters, alleging to fight for equality, breaking into stores as we speak. They will be called civil rights activists by some silver-haired legacy baby on the clown news network tonight. But they are just opportunistic criminals looking to take advantage of a vulnerable city and a thinly spread police department. You guys. The finest! I know you feel like quitting, going home, fucking . . . resigning. But think of it like this. COVID-19 and these supposedly race-fueled riots are your 911. If you look at it that way, you will find a reason to keep going and keep fighting. These restless days will define you. These moments will inform your career for decades to come. It's where your confidence and self-perception will come from. Do not give up. Trust Sergeant Sax. And the achievement of saving your city will propel you forward in your career. I turned tragedy into triumph today. I fought my battle. Can you all do the same here this morning? If we get through this, there's a big delta on the upside. We're almost home."

It was the rallying cry no one was expecting. The officers looked at one another, at once motivated by the message of the speech. If Cason was the sergeant, Jaxton was right then the lieutenant. The ten of them had sort of reset and were bonded by being there amid the boom of fireworks exploding and fires burning and about to go into the belly of the proverbial beast one last time. New York was taking a hellacious battering, but the ten counts had not yet been administered, and the championship rounds remained in this momentous bout.

CHAPTER 11

The Fragrant Fight and Kaleidoscope Colors

"At this time, within the confines of the Seventeenth Precinct, we're receiving a report of a 31 in progress. Caller states Sephora beauty products store is being burglarized. Body of the job reads 'One hundred rioters ransacking the store, stealing makeup and perfume.' Can I have some units check and advise?"

Cason turned to his squad then smiled at Jaxton. "Did she say, 'One hundred rioters?'"

"A hundred," Jaxton verified. "One zero zero."

Cason slowly raised his radio to his lips. "SRG sergeant, Central. I'm in the vicinity with my squad. Show us responding."

The officers, essentially on fumes after sixteen hours of work, gave an almost collective head nod to each other before loading up the van and heading for the store in the shadow of Rockefeller Center. They proceeded past the historical St. Patrick's Cathedral where "Fuck the Police" and "Black Lives Matter" were spray-painted in black on the lower part of the façade. The graffiti at the base of the double-spired Gothic revival church stood out like some sort of personal mutilation of New York. The doors were usually open and the nave of the church virtually invited tourists and natives alike to come inside, congregate, and worship together. The great Atlas statue, body bronze and reflecting low moonlight at this hour, still held the heavens on his shoulders across the street with a surgical mask fittingly placed over his mouth.

How art deco and Gothic revival could collide on the exact same street between quintessential examples of monolithic capitalism and monotheistic Catholicism was one of New York's greatest traits. In many ways, the structures, monuments to supposedly diametrically opposed ideas represented a similar thing: *love*. In New York, whether you loved God or money, there was a home for you. There was always a place that would welcome you. If you worshipped a divine being, if you worshipped dead presidents, if you worshipped Italian designers, there was a setting that catered to you and people just like you. Until now. They were all closed due to the virus and its punitive quarantine measures. The church, the Top of the Rock, the designer stores—all closed, authorities telling the masses it was too dangerous to go inside them while they themselves ostentatiously wined and dined. But Sephora was crowbarred wide open, and the smashed fragrance bottles had Fifth Avenue smelling like a burst of top notes.

Bergamot, lavender, lemongrass, and grapefruit wafted through the young air of daybreak. The ransackers were about to be met by nine members of the police department who had one thing in mind: going home. They may have been on their last legs, but the most dangerous fighters are desperate ones, going for the knockout.

Usually, the NYPD functions like a battalion or a brigade at events and demonstrations. But because of the chaos that had erupted across the city, the manpower was splintered and thinly spread. Firework mortars welcomed Cason's squad and ricocheted off the side of the van as they pulled up to the makeup store's overhang. Two trash can fire, ten feet apart, practically demarcated the entrance to the scene of the crime. There was a "Cannon to right of them, cannon to left of them" sort of feel as explosions cascaded, and flames raged. Jaxton, once again, raised up his cellphone to record the mayhem. He wanted to capture New York as it had rarely existed—a naked victim that was taken advantage of by pillagers. All its history and capitalistic might meant nothing right then as it was being defiled under the thinning cover of night. But the cops were on the scene, and the group of ten were all trying to prevent the glory of New York from fading permanently at the hands of the emboldened mob.

There was a little rose-pink in the sky, and Jaxton and the cops were striving to prevent that NYPD blue from fading. He was also in the home stretch of his internal battle; his once perfect life had spiraled violently out of control, but he had seemingly regained his grip on the reins. He was bridled now, it seemed; but the physical, mental, and emotional breakdown of the writer not long ago seemed imminent. He was currently going through a resurgence. It was so New York. And it was only fitting that his marathon day would end in a tumultuous confrontation in one of the most iconic streets in the United States. The denary stormed forward, including Jaxton with the ballistic helmet he borrowed and an expandable baton that he found between the seat cushions of the van. He tried to capture the faces of the marauders while capturing the moment in words in his mind.

"My name is Jaxton Bello," he stated on camera. "I was a writer for *Metropolis Adjacent*, and I am composing an independent piece on protests in New York. I am recording as we speak, and I'm encouraging all of you to put down the merchandise and put your hands behind your backs."

Jaxton needed a megaphone. He was ignored except for a fragrance bottle that sailed through the air and bounced off the top of his helmet.

"Fuck you, fascist!" yelled a young Indian American female with leather makeup bags under each arm.

"Guys, everybody here is under for burglary. We have probable cause on every single one of these assholes. Grab whoever you can!" Cason barked out.

The rabble became more enraged at the sight of the police. They punched and kicked the officers who were now swinging rods in defense. The cops were under siege as a dense mass of men and women attempted to pummel them. Jaxton put his phone away and swung his borrowed expandable baton like a battle-axe. He was punched on the chin, and he swung wildly, eyes closed, splitting one shoplifter's chin wide open.

"Holy fucking shit!" he marveled at his own fury. "Are you okay?"

The men and women in blue were agents of the state and the embodiment of the very entity the looters wanted to abolish. "Defund the police" had spontaneously become a mantra in America, a rallying cry for the progressives looking to overcompensate for the tragic police-involved deaths by dismantling the entire system. The police were somehow seen as the enemy by many—racists despite so many of them being people of color and corrupt despite most of them following the law and police procedures to the letter. The insurrection taking place was further ignited by the presence of the law enforcement agents. They were essentially accelerants in this microcosmic battle in the perfume shop. This was ironic as they were desperately trying to put out the actual flames with small, inadequate department-issued fire extinguishers.

"Cason, are you good?" Jaxton surveyed, scanning for anyone that he could perceive as a threat to his well-being.

"I'm fucking good. You better swing that nightstick, buddy! I saved your life once already today. You better get self-reliant really quick."

Makeup was pulverizing in the air, coloring the officers in pastel colors. Their uniforms never looked so polychromatic; golds, yellows, and pinks adorning that iconic NYPD Navy. Officers, severely extended past even a double shift now, never smelled better as protesters used fragrance bottles as impromptu grenades. Each explosion of glass, and the aroma it released, further infuriated the overtired officers. Billy club strikes were heard, incapacitating the violators on impact. A bloody pile of arrestees began to form as four officers set up a blue wall to prevent them from escaping. This image crystallized the dilemma playing out as so many of the city's citizens slept. There was chaos and bloodshed, and there was law and order trying to prevail. A tall dark-skinned cop, Officer Justice, ironically, approached the sergeant in the middle of the melee.

"Hey, boss, what do you want us to do with the collars?" he asked, resembling a human kaleidoscope.

"Just leave them there and get back in this fight," Cason instructed.

Officer Justice stood six foot two inches tall and had an effortless, almost a glide to his gait. He smoothly moved back to his position when a looter attempted to bowl him over to flee. Justice lifted him up and launched the assailant, back first, onto a makeup counter. Mascaras, bronzers, and application brushes scattered in the air. Makeup mirrors fragmented as foundations and blushes spun on the floor.

"That's what you fucking get," Justice taunted angrily in his raspy voice, "you fuckin' perp, trying to take *me* out?"

Another young freedom fighter jumped on the officer's back and placed his forearm under his chin, across his windpipe. Officer Justice bent his knees, tucked his chin, and flipped him over his shoulders. The young man somersaulted onto a fragrance counter, clearing out all woodsy colognes. The cacophonous sounds of glass bottles breaking and young adults crying made for an unforgettable symphony for anybody in attendance.

Jaxton turned to Cason, who was fighting off his own insurgents while simultaneously supervising his squad.

"Is this what you were expecting?" Cason asked, frantically looking over his shoulder.

"I've learned to expect the unexpected with you," Jaxton returned. "I've been wanting to hang out with you at night but maybe not during a riot."

"Riot? Blasphemer. The phrase is civil disobedience," Cason corrected. "Mind your euphemisms."

"What was I thinking?"

"And I don't think your wife approves of you and me reliving the past, Jax."

"I know. You can't have one foot in the past and one in the future," Jaxton replied.

"Duck!" Cason commanded as a perfume bottle smashed against a large, illuminated mirror.

"Can we finish this conversation later, Case?"

"I thought writers were supposed to be good multitaskers?"

Skirmishes surrounded them, but the NYPD appeared to be regaining control of matters.

"I have an idea for a headline tomorrow . . .," Jaxton began.

"NYPD kicks mostly peaceful protesters asses?" Cason responded.

"You and your team are going to be depicted as heavy-handed colonizers."

"Colonizers?" Cason refuted. "I've got kids from actual colonized countries in my squad going up against privileged brats stealing mascara because they feel 'oppressed.' This is some stupid, ass-backward shit."

Cason and his squad slugged it out with the trespassers raiding the retail store. Jaxton got his licks in, digging in his heels and waving his borrowed rod at attackers. He had placed his life in harm's way and was, currently, an honorary member of the police department. He felt so alive. He climbed onto a counter to get a bird's eye view of the fracas. It was exhilarating being up there. It was like being in the mezzanine for a Broadway show during its climax or like he was back up on the steel eagles of the Chrysler building with the wind on his face. He could see Officer Jean depositing rioters on the cashier side of checkout counters. It was a battle between officers and criminals staged in the most unlikely of venues.

It would later be characterized as a battle between Blue Lives Matter and Black Lives Matter, but it had nothing to do with color, even as colors filled the air from the detonated makeup palettes. Blue Lives Matter was an appropriate response to the assassinations of police but was viewed, somehow, as contesting the fact that black lives matter. Black lives were extremely important to the NYPD, much more so than to politicians who used the phrase to their perceived political advantage. Some officers laid down their own lives, protecting the lives of black men and women. Some of those officers were black themselves. But that political organization's opposition to the police and its quest for abolition made it difficult for the cops to openly support both. When given a choice, people will always side with what puts food on the table, not that which is trying to remove it by way of an absurd defunding movement. This created the chasm that was effectively playing out on Fifth Avenue as the clock struck 5:30 a.m. All the while, an ingénue congresswoman, who supported the destructive policy, slept peacefully in her silk sheets, ready to rise and chirp about inequality from a one-thousand-dollar device.

"SRG sergeant, Central," Cason stated with authority into his cracked radio.

"SRG sergeant, proceed," the dispatcher acknowledged.

"Let me get a paddy wagon to the corner of Fifth Avenue and West Forty-Seventh Street. We're going to have multiple arrests. I have some officers and some perps injured as well, so let me get multiple buses to this location."

"10-04, SRG sergeant. What's the nature of the injuries and how many buses?" she followed up.

Cason took inventory of the landscape and could hardly believe what he saw. It was a scene of human carnage unlike any that he had witnessed in his career besides September 11. Looters, assaulting blockading officers in their attempt to escape, had been disciplined with billy clubs. There were ample amounts of blood in the aisles of the store. His squad had various bumps, bruises, and lacerations to show for their efforts.

"Central, we have people with head injuries over here. We have officers with hand injuries. I've got officers suffering from exhaustion. Just send as many buses as you can, please," Cason requested.

Some looters made it out with makeup kits and fragrances; the officers were not going to chase them for it. There were enough arrestees in custody already and almost too many for the officers to safely handle.

"Was this your battle of Gettysburg?" Jaxton asked, his hand on his rapidly expanding chest.

"This was my battle of I don't know what. The fragrant fight or some shit," Cason coined.

"The fragrance fight. I like that. Do you think the mayor's office is sending anyone to handle the contact training for this incident?"

"Oh, contact tracing! Yeah sure. The mayor himself is doing it."

"Trace *this*," Jaxton replied.

When the day began, the narrative had shifted from the deadly pandemic to police brutality and systemic racism. Now, the meta stories of group violence, looting, and arson as a response to social injustice would begin to take shape. But it was never properly condemned by elected officials and would reach its horrific low point during the insurrection at the US Capitol on January 6. Ancillary issues would be tacked on and would further polarize the American citizens. There would be so much unrest in the streets over the next few weeks all throughout the nation. Images of American flags in flames, storefront windows being demolished, merchandise looted in the name of Black Lives Matter would be something that many Americans found troubling despite their support for the initial cause. Some members of the organization would call the looting reparations as if one could somehow link a designer handbag to the centuries-long institution of slavery. None of those details seemed to matter now.

"You guys kick some serious ass," Jaxton let out. "Is the department hiring right now? I'm ready to take the oath."

"I don't think you'd pass the psych test, brother. You with a gun?"

"Come on, man. Too soon, too soon!" Jaxton replied, jabbing light punches at Cason's midsection.

"Are you fucking pigs going to transport us to the bookings or just suck each other off all day?" asked a young man in a Che Guevara T-shirt. "You fucking Uncle Tom sellouts."

"The guy on your shirt was a racist and a homophobe. People don't usually wear their biases so openly. I'm glad you did though, little man," Jaxton replied.

"Fuck you, pig!" the young man spouted.

"I'm not a pig. I'm a journalist. That's worse right now, I think."

"Someone escort Napoleon to the front of the line," Cason ordered, guiding the arrestee by the shoulder.

"Ah! The handcuffs are too tight!" he complained.

"Of course, you would say that. Just go," Cason ordered.

"I have asthma, man. I can't breathe!"

"You were able to breathe when you were stealing Gucci colognes," Jaxton quipped.

"That was Versace."

"I think we have our first confession," Cason announced.

The scene of young people being led out of the store in chains was a powerful one. The turret lights of responding vehicles and the yelp of the sirens were jarring as if the war that had just transpired was not jarring enough. New York had, once again, emerged as a strangely paradoxical city. It was still as diverse as the diverse line of criminals being led out of the beauty supply store in daisy chains. But it was uniform in that they all acted in precisely the same manner and complained about the exact same thing: the handcuffs. The gang would not be held long anyway as Bail Reform had created the ultimate revolving door, releasing them the next day to transgress again.

These riots proved that you could not reap the benefits of so-called criminal justice reform without bearing the costs. Retail stores had been used as ground zero in the battle to topple what they believed to be evil, oppressive capitalism. All the country's ills and inequities were attributed to the economic system that came to dominate the planet. Somehow, socialism, genocidal in its implementation, was perceived as the advantageous way to proceed by a generation of misinformed youths wearing the face of an Argentine Marxist revolutionary on their pullovers.

"Justice, you'll make sure everybody is good," Cason asked his senior officer.

"I got you, boss. We'll make sure all the arresting officers can articulate the circumstances of the arrest and that we have enough details for the DAs to prosecute."

"Thanks, brother. You're my driver for a reason," Cason complimented.

"No doubt, Sarge," he replied smoothly.

"You see? My guys are self-motivated," Cason bragged.

"Your guys really are incredible. I cannot believe what I just witnessed. I mean that was absolutely crazy!" Jaxton exclaimed.

"It's like that sometimes," Cason stated with a grin before unzipping his patrol bag. "Are you too beat to smoke one of these?" he asked, pulling out two hand-rolled coffee-flavored cigars from a family-owned shop in the Gun Hill section of the Bronx.

"Is that the cigar I owe you?"

"Now you owe me two, Jax."

"I think I owe you a lot more than just two stogies," Jaxton asserted.

"Should I light you up? The Havana I mean . . ."

"I caught that. I don't really do this anymore, but . . . this had to be the most tumultuous day of my entire life," Jaxton acknowledged. "Might as well conclude it with a celebratory cigar. We're going to burn it right here?"

"Not right here. Right there," Cason revealed, turning his head to an imposing monument south of where they stood vertically puncturing the sky and letting out the rays of the new day.

"Shall we check for King Kong?"

"What could possibly go wrong?" Cason said through a smile that practically wanted to tempt fate again.

And the two proceeded to Thirty-Fourth Street and to the cloud-reaching needle in the center of Midtown South for an after-party reminiscent of their younger, more exultant years.

CHAPTER 12

Empire State of Being

Cason drove his friend to the Empire State Building, and the security officer in front of the edifice waved the two of them in. Conceived in the giddy aftermath of the Roaring Twenties, the structure still enforced capitalistic muscle one hundred years later. The galvanizing gold atrium symbolized the paragon of art deco.

Jaxton could not help but become a tourist of the landmark, marveling at the ceiling murals made of aluminum and gold leaf, the lobby's luminous starbursts, and its Nero Marquina marble. It was as if Jaxton and Cason wanted to spite the protestors and celebrate at a venue that embodied what that the faction had been conditioned to hate: America. The American ingenuity that caused cities to explode and then grow vertically was now believed by some boisterous minority to represent bigotry and oppression. Jaxton and Cason did not subscribe to that way of thinking, and so they rode the elevator to the eighty-sixth floor for an oft-postponed celebratory smoke. The two were lured onto the observation deck by a breathtaking yellow-orange sunrise.

"My god, look at that," Cason admired, squinting his eyes before proceeding to slice off the tip of his cigar with a monogrammed guillotine cutter.

"That is one beautiful sight. It's like a shot to the lungs," Jaxton praised.

The two took in the majestic daybreak while inhaling the invigorating air in between puffs of the coffee-flavored tobacco.

"What a day," Cason began.

"What a day. It's about to be literally a day, twenty-four hours," Jaxton remarked, "Twenty-four hours away from Grace and Waverly. I miss them dearly. I can't believe what I did, and I mean *everything* that I did today . . . and yesterday. I can't believe how this all started. I can't believe I almost never saw them again. If not for you . . . if not for you . . .I . . ."

Jaxton struggled to give credit as tears began to pool in his puffy eyes.

"You would have done the same thing for me, my friend. I didn't do anything special."

"You saved my life, Case'."

"Like I said, that's nothing spec—"

"Oh, screw you," Jaxton said, laughing and wiping his nose with his wrist. "My life matters."

"Don't say that. Watch it! You can't say your life matters. That's racist."

"It's crazy," Jaxton said softly. "People are arguing over whose life matters. How did we get to this absurd point?"

"I don't know. Maybe you and I will never understand," Cason deduced. "Maybe we just need to shut up and support the cause."

"I don't know about that. The cause got you sent to the hospital tonight. It's hard to support that. That was carnage. I wonder how much of the city got destroyed?" Jaxton inquired.

"I don't know. A significant portion for sure. We were definitely caught with our pants down."

"So we can agree that these were historic acts of vandalism against this city, right?"

"Yeah, I would say so. Absolutely," Cason replied. "Why? Do you own stocks in insurance companies or something?"

"You know me," Jaxton coyly returned.

"Yeah, I do know you. You're writing something aren't you?"

"I've been writing since the day began. Up here," he stated, pointing to his temple.

"Everybody loves a comeback story," Cason replied. "Go for it. Another bestseller. It'll get you out of your financial hole."

"Right . . . At what time is the mayor's press conference?"

"Not sure. The mayor isn't too concerned about the destruction. The inspector said he called Police Plaza and ordered us to treat the protesters with kid gloves."

"Shit if those baton shots were kid gloves, I'd hate to see you guys when the gloves are off," Jaxton quipped.

"People don't understand. We're a reactive department. We only respond to the level of force that we're met with. You want to bring sticks and bricks to a demonstration then we'll meet you at that level. It was either unleash the nightsticks or my entire squad ends up in the hospital with head injuries, so . . . Once your life is on the line, any mayor trying to call shots from his ivory tower with a police detail is completely irrelevant. He wants to use kid gloves? He can come here and suppress these riots with Mickey Mouse gloves himself."

"Yeah," Jaxton nodded, "I agree. It's easy to tell someone how to do something when you yourself are unaffected by it. He's an elitist."

"You see my point," Cason tersely replied before pausing for a moment and reflecting. "You know, a smart person once said, 'We will probably be judged not by the monuments we build but by the monuments we destroyed.'"

"Yeah. That was Ada Louise Huxtable." Jaxton thought about the ethos of that statement and the scope of it in the larger sense. "She was right. And we really suck as a society right now. We currently have a population of grown men and women pissed off at statues. George Washington, Christopher Columbus, Abraham freaking Lincoln, suddenly they're public enemies. It's bizarre. Hey, speaking of dead guys. How did you know I was going to be at the George Washington Bridge this morning? That's the question I've been meaning to ask you all day."

"Come on, brother. You have tells."

"I have tells?"

"Yeah, you're so lyrical. Everything with you is telling a story, weaving a narrative, and making intellectual associations. You do it all the time . . ."

"Okay . . ."

"Okay, so we were talking about the upcoming election, and I asked you what you thought about the two candidates and you replied—"

"They're both subpar. The only president I care about is the first," Jaxton finished.

"Exactly. You know then. You gave it away," Cason revealed. "Then you said, 'I'm about to do something monumental that's gonna make a big splash.' Monuments . . . splash . . . first president . . . I didn't need Google for that. If that's not tipping your hand, nothing is. I saw it for what it was, a cry for help."

"It was a cry for help. And you listened. Just like you listened to Life on that rooftop. You have a gift for listening."

"Yeah, well . . . that's only part of it. What comes after? Life killed himself two days later when I wasn't working. It's my biggest regret. The cops said he asked for me."

"Of course, he asked for you."

"I'm going to keep a close eye on you. Don't be surprised if you see me more often."

"I don't think that's necessary."

"I wasn't asking. I could never let that happen again."

Jaxton would have to rebuild. And it would also take the maltreated metropolis considerable time to repair the damage and even more time to recover from the financial toll. From the eighty-sixth story observation deck, the two men gazed out at the sun as it reclaimed the sky above a completely changed cultural, economic, and physical New York landscape. They drew in the essences from their cigars to almost intoxicating effect and blew out tendrils of smoke into the newly birthed daytime atmosphere. Their energy seemed to wane despite the air trying its best to invigorate them. The two men appeared to retreat into themselves and reminisce about their shared paths. From the inebriating heights of their professional ascents in 2010s to the death-scraping lows escorted by the coronavirus and almost flatlining on the George Washington Bridge, the pair appeared to journey through their consciousness reciprocally. They wore their thoughts heavily and slumped on the guardrail of the mammoth symbol of the Land of Opportunity's strength.

"You know you don't realize that certain periods in your life change the way you smile. You physically smile differently. It's like it takes the luster off you, steals your light kind of. My daughter is the singular thing I kept thinking about today. The one thing that kept me from slipping back into that dark place where you found me. She kept reaching for me," Jaxton confessed. "How could a child, a small, innocent . . . tender child, hold a grown man together like glue?"

Cason just stared at his friend, who was pouring out his heart at the semi-pinnacle of America's favorite skyscraper.

"They say it's lonely at the top," Cason reminded while looking down at the city.

"Sometimes, the top feels so much like the bottom," Jaxton replied. "I need to go, man. I need to go home and hug them and kiss them and love them," he stated with his voice breaking into pieces.

He took one strong pull from his cigar, which suddenly stood as a timer tallying the minutes between him and his Odyssean return home. "I need to feel Grace's adorable little body in my arms again."

"I could have someone drive you. I'll make sure you actually get there this time."

"That would be great. I'm dying to hear her infectious 'Dad-dy.' I just want to feel her gentle hug and hear her breathing into my ear. Everything would be alleviated just by holding her in my arms," Jaxton disclosed, pantomiming a hug.

Jaxton put out his smoke, and Cason extinguished his.

"You ready?"

"I'm ready, brother. I've waited a lifetime for this moment."

Cason radioed for a police car to pick up his friend at the foot of the high-rise. The operator turned on the turret lights, and blue and red spun centrifugally, far less striking against the light of new day than the cloak of deep night.

"You might want to put your seat belt on," Officer Concepcion suggested as he humorously revved up the engine.

"What's a seat belt?" Jaxton deadpanned.

"Enough said," the officer replied before speeding off with Jaxton in the passenger seat absent any safety devices or harnesses.

The RMP made a sharp U-turn and ripped westbound across the vast expanse of Thirty-Fourth Street. The Macy's Believe sign, unilluminated, gradually disappeared as they sped past it. Jaxton still read it and saw it as an omen of hope and optimism for the days ahead.

They soon zoomed up the Henry Hudson Parkway and past the iconic neighborhoods of the Upper West Side, Harlem, and Washington Heights. Over four hundred years before, the eponymous explorer had touched down in North America on behalf of the Dutch East India Company, unaware of the transcendent civilization that would ignite by his matchstick. As Hudson surveyed what would become the modern New York metropolitan area, he likely never concluded that the concept of a city would come to be and that it would one day grow into the greatest society of all time. Jaxton climbed his way up to the zenith of that society before an Icarian fall. And now he longingly rode another iconic figure, Robert Moses's, famous public works project to his sanctuary-like abode.

From Ammann's massive connector to Shreve, Lamb, and Harmon's historic edifice, to Moses's famed parkway, to a humble colonial four-bedroom house in Yorktown Heights, Jaxton was nearing the end of his journey. All truths would be told once he stepped through the threshold of that house. Everything left in his life was left at that address. It was the conclusion to the longest day and the beginning of his new life. As the police vehicle jetted through the tolls on the Hudson Bridge, Jaxton was feeling Ulysses-like as home approached. To have come so far from depths so low, through painful memories and sky-reaching triumphs, Jaxton sprinted out of the radio motor patrol car, house keys in hand, and hurtled toward the front door. He deftly inserted the key, twisted it, and pushed the gate seemingly in one motion. He nearly crashed through the front entrance, but the barrel bolt was engaged, and he would have to summon Waverly to enter. He pulled out his mobile device, 1 percent of the phone battery life remaining, and called his one remaining lifeline.

"Hello?" Waverly answered, freshly exiting her dream.

"I'm outside," Jaxton revealed.

"You're outside?" she repeated groggily. "Oh my god. You're outside!"

She made the short trip from their bedroom to the front door, internally questioning why it had taken him so long for him to arrive home.

"What time is it?" she asked.

"It's seven something . . ."

As he completed saying "something," something that he thought he would never see again walked past the one curtainless window and struck his retina as it did five years ago, filling his sight with iridescent color. She slowly opened the door, her opposite hand shielding her drowsy face from the inspired morning sun.

"Wow," Jaxton exhaled, the door sweeping inward into the world he thought he had permanently left behind.

He could almost relive the colorful moments of the vertical collage of family photos adorning the living room wall as he stood, an outsider, on the welcome mat of his home.

"Come in, baby," Waverly invited, slightly more frigidly than would be expected.

Jaxton held her with all the strength left in his unnourished body. He prolonged the affection. It was reminiscent of their first embrace but with a lifetime of history woven into it. Jaxton was now an explorer returning to civilization from the wilderness.

"I miss you," he whispered, tucking her shoulder closer into him with his chin. He shook her gently as if trying to galvanize their love.

"You missed me you said?" she asked, slightly louder than he did.

"*Miss* you. Present tense," he clarified. "I miss you. I miss *us*."

"We're right here, my love."

"Are we? You said some powerful words."

"Oh, Jaxton, you're still harping on that? People say things when they're upset," she downplayed, breaking the embrace. "It's not the end of the world."

"It can be. Words have consequences. That's what you would always tell me, right?"

"So do actions," she replied.

"Oftentimes words provoke actions."

Jaxton possessed a profound love for his wife but had just concluded an emotional marathon through his past and barely made it to the present. It was not necessarily a finish line that he crossed. He had survived the gauntlet but had arrived home the worse for wear and with certain matters still unsettled. "How much do you push forward? How much do you protect what lies behind?" were questions at the forefront of his clouded mind. He had to find a resolution between the concrete and the abstract, the fleeting and the enduring in a way that made sense. Since their marriage, their emotional journeys were avowed to chart parallel courses but had grown, at times, more divergently. Like spindly branches of a bough growing in disagreeing directions. He slowly walked through the house, and she turned on a light switch to make things more visible for him since the navy-blue blackout curtains on the other side were performing their function well.

"Is that makeup on you?" she asked.

"Oh, yeah. I thought I got it all off," he fumbled. "Is Grace still asleep?"

"Yes, she's in her crib—What do you mean you thought you got it all off? So you're not denying you have makeup on you?"

"I'm not denying anything right now. I was in a big brawl in a . . . in a beauty store. People were rioting, and they were looting all the fragrances and makeup sets, and they were smashing them all over the place."

"'People were rioting in a makeup store' is the alibi you're going to go with?" she interrogated, hands firmly on hips.

"Yes, that's right," he affirmed.

"And they were breaking fragrances, but you don't smell like any fragrances?" she asked with steely ire. "That's an impressive dodge."

"Maybe the cigar smoke killed it. I'm so tired I can't even smell right now. But I am almost certain that a bottle of Flowerbomb exploded on me."

"You were smoking cigars? I thought you quit. Wow. No shame in incriminating yourself. Walking in here covered in some girl's makeup like it's perfectly normal because you were 'working on a story.'"

"The makeup on my clothes is not some girl's makeup. It is some *company's* makeup. Clinique or Lancôme or I don't know that many makeup makers per se. We were all covered in it. You can call Cason—"

"Oh, so that's who you were smoking the cigar with? Was it in the emergency room or outside of it? Is he still single? Or is he back with that stripper?"

"I don't think she does that anymore . . ."

"What was it, Jaxton? Like back in your glory days?" she pestered.

"It was nothing like the glory days. It was war. I was out at first, searching for something, but not with Cason. And then I was with Cason, but it was to cover the protests. Then the protests became riots," he explained. "Hey, imagine there was no tomorrow."

"You're always so melodramatic. This conversation is done," she concluded before leaving behind a few choice expletives.

"No—baby, calm down. I love you. I kept my promise," Jaxton said, tiring.

He finally surrendered, throwing both hands in the air. He was upset by Waverly, even more so because he abhorred his transgressions with Adriana. Conversely, it seemed he loved himself again, and that was a trade that he would have to make in the moment as a matter of necessity. It would keep him pressing forward. But some things you can reconcile and others you cannot. The sound of Waverly's words trailed off as he removed both his shoes and entered his daughter's room.

The creaking of the door covered in My Little Pony decals slightly awoke the child but not in a way that caused her precious brown eyes to open. Jaxton hunched over and admired her there as she just breathed in her crib. Her belly rising and falling assured him that she was healthy, safe, and sound. It was the most reassuring sight he could see in the entire world. He hooked his messenger bag on the crib headboard and shed his shirt, stained in so many ways, the Austin 3:16 on it badly peeling. He really did come quite far, from depths both dark and low to sky-grazing highs and explosive crashes. But he made it home. He placed the *Wicked* snow globe on the railing of the crib and wound up its turnkey. A drowsing melody was freed from the commemorative ornament. Jaxton traveled all this way to climb into a crib with a toddler, his precious little girl.

He nimbly maneuvered into the crib and found a small piece of real estate to curl into, slightly scooting his daughter's small body over a few inches. He hung the *Starry Night* ornament off the remnants of Grace's old Care Bears mobile. The sound of the music box and the spin of Van Gogh's swirls twirling by a string created calm. And peace. He put his arm over Grace and squeezed her gently. As small as she was, she was as big as anything in the world. The world was upside down, and Grace currently held his upside-down life together like a linchpin. But he still had his life, and that was his great triumph today. It would ostensibly be his new starting point.

Jaxton yearned to return to a world before the virus, before the police killings, before the riots, before recrossing paths with Adriana, before his vicious fight with Waverly and 7:00 a.m. on the George Washington Bridge. All this time, Grace was his guiding light home, a miniature compass in unicorn pajamas. The light that kept him on the guided path, preventing him from slipping, perhaps literally, into a ditch. The writer had come back from ruins, but was he himself ruined? And right then, Jaxton lay there. He simply lay there. She lay with him. He forgot the rest of the world existed.

And then the darkness came for him again.

Jaxton blinked and a damn burst from his shut eyes. He began to tremble, the mattress rumbling as he held the shard of glass that he picked up off the street in his fingertips. He tightened his grip on the fragment and brought the glass piece to his opposite wrist. This was the bridge all over again. But there was no Cason there to stop him now. The *Wicked* souvenir's melody was expiring, the last few notes trickling out. Then the music stopped. Jaxton applied pressure to his wrist, not quite puncturing his skin yet.

And then Grace giggled in her sleep. The sound surprising him after everything had gone soundless. Now he could hear Waverly taking out some pans in the kitchen for a breakfast he would not taste. The tears slalomed down his stubbly cheek as he held Grace with his free hand. He leaned over to see her precious dreaming face. Her lips were curled upward at the corners. She emitted small, delightful sounds that only a toddler could. Everything, all the emotions, came out of him in that crib and onto the twin-sized mattress and Grace's pajamas. Grace continued smiling as she dreamt. This caused Jaxton to unfurl a wet smile. Three years on Earth, and Grace's life was a happy one. And he, right then and there, committed to keeping it that way.

Jaxton lobbed the glass piece out of the crib unambivalently. The future would prevail. Jaxton became his own hero. He reset the snow globe's turnkey and let the music box renew its sweet melody. It played so softly and tenderly, and he placed his head gently upon the pillow. He did not utter a single, solitary sound. This was his great silent roar, and he sought to share it with the world and feel its fingertips on his newly bared soul.

The Great Silent Roar by Jaxton Bello.

Printed in the USA
CPSIA information can be obtained
at www.ICGtesting.com
CBHW031233030824
12481CB00030B/206